EAGLE HEART

SHONA BLASS

GOLD CROW BOOKS

Published in 2021 by Gold Crow Books

ISBN 978-1-8382554-0-4 (paperback)
ISBN 978-1-8382554-1-1 (e-book)

British Library Cataloguing in Publication Data
A CIP catalogue record for this book is available
from the British Library

Cover design and typesetting by JD Smith Design

For Paul

CHAPTER 1

What about my father? My thoughts spin, my hand starts shaking, my breath quickens. I can't take my eyes off my phone: 'Breaking News – Disciples Attack Colchester House.' I need to stay calm, but my heart's racing. It's two thirty in the afternoon. I'm sitting in Coffee Primo. It's possible everything will be different after this moment but nobody else seems affected. My colleagues, Magda and Ollie, are chatting behind the counter. There are only a few customers about and I'm taking a late lunch. Outside, snow is beginning to fall.

I try to read on but I'm struggling. There's a picture of Colchester House: an iconic image of the security facility, round in shape, a concrete fortress. I shiver. It's not called 'The Jelly Mould' for nothing. The Disciples have done what shouldn't be possible. They've breached its security doors and released some of the prisoners. Recently, the authorities were congratulating themselves on neutralising the eco-terrorist group. Not now. It's the Disciples' most audacious attack. There's no other information. Not yet.

I look up. The snow outside is falling faster. Who would carry out an attack in these conditions? But they've done it. I text Charley and Flint; my sister and cousin have got to see this.

Flint responds in seconds. 'Stay cool.' Does that mean he doesn't think I am – or maybe he's not either?

Charley texts. 'Can't look now.' She's a photographer's assistant and loves her job; she won't mess up. I realise my right leg is bobbing up and down. I can barely sit still.

Fifteen minutes of my lunch break left. I try to finish my toasted panini but it sticks in my throat. It's hard to drink my cappuccino. I can't think straight so focus on the snow. It will be freezing when I get back tonight and the landlord's a bastard – he's not fixed the heating. There'll be six of us in that house shivering our butts off.

Lunch ends and I go back to making coffees. Rush hour sweeps in and the customers increase. I don't have time to glance at my phone so excuse myself and go to the toilet. I can't stay long but I have to read more. Grainy CCTV footage has been posted online. Four masked Disciples filing past a security door and moving down a corridor. I play it several times. And he's among them. Gil Zimmerman, the Disciples' leader. His face is covered but I know his build, slim and muscular, and the way he moves. It's burnt on my memory. I can barely breathe.

'Hey.' Someone's at the door. 'We need you out here.' It's Ollie.

I pocket my phone and go back and join them.

Later, when we close up, I take the rubbish bags round the back and throw them in the industrial bins. The alleyway is private, the snow untouched. Hidden, I get out my phone. There's more information. The three prisoners who escaped are named, their mugshots shown: Marilyn Jenkins, who looks mean; John Brisbane, who the police warn the public not to approach, he's got a history of violence; and Brian Minster. My eyes cloud as I look at the photo. Brian Minster – the traitor. The scientist who tried to release secrets of national security. His eyes look cold, deadened. I hate that picture. And I'm crying. I'm eighteen years old and I'm crying like a child. I wipe my face, relieved that the snow's disguising my tears. Brian Minster, my father, is free.

I leave the station and trudge through the snow. Ahead, our house share looks a wreck. The outside's ingrained with dirt, the curtains don't fit the draughty windows and the rubbish bins have been raided by a fox. I struggle to call it home, that word belongs to the house we lived in with Dad, but it's better than the youth hostels and shelters we've stayed in.

Spider and Jez are in the kitchen. I go to put on the kettle.

'It's freezing out there,' I say. 'I'm going to try and run a bath.'

Jez looks at me with disdain. 'Are you under the illusion there's hot water in this place?'

I shrug. 'I'll try anyway.' Really, I want to speak to Charley and Flint, but if they're not back yet I'll be alone with my thoughts. 'I take it you haven't seen Sophie or Jake?' I ask, using their cover names.

Spider shrugs, no.

I go upstairs. The water that comes out the bath tap is barely warm. If I get in I'll probably turn blue, but somehow I don't mind. I'll numb. I lock the bathroom door and strip. The mirror above the sink has a crack in the corner, but I still see my reflection clearly. Pale skin, slim build, mousy-coloured hair and blue eyes. And then the scar near my left shoulder. A bullet wound. It went in the front of me and came out the back. It was over a year ago but it's still sensitive to touch.

I get in the bath. The water is cold but I submerge myself completely. I lie as flat as I can on the bottom, and then I breathe. Bubbles rise from my mouth. I laugh but only for a moment. More bubbles. I breathe deeply and think of my father. Tears start coming again.

I'm linked to Dad through my body forever. Through the genetic mutation he gave us, Charley and I can breathe underwater for hours if necessary. And I'm linked by his involvement with the Disciples. The wound in my shoulder aches. I see Gil in that corridor again, and my tears are tears of rage.

A loud knock at the door.

I sit up quickly. 'Hey, I'm in the bath.'

'It's me,' Flint says. 'Thought I'd let you know Soph and I are back but I gotta leave for work soon.'

I get out of the bath and dry quickly, dress and go into their room. We've told everyone we're old friends from school so I don't go into their room often – it wouldn't look right – but now it's too important. My twin Charley is sitting on the double bed. Her long hair flows over her shoulders and her face is serious. Flint's near the window. His soft afro hair is cropped tight to his head and his dark skin stands out against his white shirt; the sleeves are rolled up revealing his tattoos, a mix of Celtic and other tribal-looking patterns. He dresses well for work – he's a bouncer. I close the door behind me. We're normally relaxed with each other but the news is a shock.

'It's hard to believe,' I whisper. 'I'm finding it very hard to believe but … Dad's free.' The words feel strange on my tongue.

'Free?' Flint says softly. 'Well, he's not in Colchester House.'

'Which is a good thing,' I say.

He shrugs, unsure.

I turn to my sister. 'I don't know what to think, Dom.' Her blue eyes hold mine. 'I just keep worrying about what kind of state he's in, given what MI5 have done to him … two years of being locked up.' She wavers, upset. 'He might not be alright at all, and now he's with the Disciples. What will they do with him?'

'I … I think they'll look after him,' I say carefully. 'Given what they've done to free him, I trust they'll look after him.'

'Trust?' Charley says, bemused. 'No, Dom. Gil Zimmerman is not someone you trust.'

We're quiet. I hate the tension between us.

'Do you think we're still safe?' I ask.

'Hopefully,' Flint says. At least he's staying calm. 'We've not been in the news for ages, and I can't see we will now. The only people they're gonna go after are the Disciples. We just need to keep our cool and carry on as we are: Jake, Soph and Luke.'

'I keep feeling there's something we should do,' I say.

'There's nothing,' Flint says.

'But there must be. I want to see him.'

Silence.

'*Dom, don't do this,*' Charley whispers into my head. Flint can't hear her.

I look down.

'Don't think that, Dom,' Flint says gently. 'It won't help.'

'Dad's free.'

'No, Dom,' Charley says aloud. 'Dad's not free. He's with the Disciples – that's not freedom. We, *you,*' she stresses, 'almost died getting away from them. So you can't see him, none of us can, not until he's really free. And that means he's not with the Disciples, he's not with MI5, he's just free, and I don't know when or if that's ever going to happen.'

She's crying. The lump at the back of my throat aches. When I can speak again, I try to sound calm. 'So what … we need to forget him and ignore what's happened?'

'Course you can't forget him,' Flint says. 'And right now we're upset. This brings up shit from the past. But that doesn't mean we can do anything but watch what happens.'

I look at him and feel bewildered. '*Charley, there must be something,*' I beg into her thoughts.

'*Stop, Dom.*' She shakes her head then says aloud, 'I actually feel sick. He's probably in more danger now than he was in Colchester House. At least we knew where he was then.'

I don't understand her; our thoughts and feelings can be so in tune. Why can't she see what I do?

I leave their room and go into mine. I lock the door and take a few deep breaths. Slowly, I crouch down and carefully dislodge a loose floorboard beneath my bed. I put my hand into the cavity and fumble about. I touch cold hard metal. A gun. The pistol Gil held to my head then gave me. I haven't touched it since we first moved in. Charley and Flint wanted to throw it in the Thames.

'No,' I said, 'he gave it to me, and I'm not ready to lose it yet.'

Now, I feel a strange kind of relief knowing it's still there.

CHAPTER 2

The next day, I make coffees at work but all I can think of is Dad. There are so many questions I want answered. What is he like now? Is he traumatised? 'Everyone's got their breaking point,' Gil once said. And what happens next? Charley and Flint may be right – we're safe and there's nothing we can do – but the possibility of seeing him again …

The morning rush of customers slows and I go to clear some tables. I leave Ollie and Magda to gossip behind the counter. I'm finding it hard to hide how preoccupied I am. Normally, I'm good at chatting with them. We'll talk about anything and have a laugh. Magda, my manager, likes to tell stories about her husband and daughter, and family back in Poland. She's always trying to make the world better.

'Mother Magda,' Ollie calls her. 'Mother Magda loves to look after her boys,' he'll say with a wink, referring to the two of us.

It's true, she's like that. I cracked a joke at my interview, and swear I got the job because it made her laugh.

Ollie's not much older than me, but he's convinced he knows a lot more about life. He went through a tough time coming out and thinks that gives him a greater understanding of people and society.

'Not everybody lives such an easy life as you, Luke,' he likes to tell me.

But really, it's great, because neither of them has a clue.

I finish wiping down tables and go and join them.

'Ollie's got a new boyfriend,' Magda says proudly.

'Oh, yeah?' I turn to him.

'Oh, yeah,' he says grinning. 'I am having fun!'

I haven't seen him so happy.

'Now all we've got to do is find you someone, Luke.' Magda smiles.

I decide not to tell her finding a girlfriend is the last thing on my mind.

Lunchtime and I go out. I've limited time so I need to be quick. I've got a distance to walk. I hurry down block after block then turn into a street I normally avoid. Immediately, my heart begins to race; I'm like the victim of a crime returning to the scene. A Café Terrazza comes into view. It's a rival coffee chain but I go inside. I keep my eyes focused ahead, but my peripheral vision picks up the customers sitting with their LifeStar Corporation security cards hanging from their necks. I buy a hot chocolate and sit at the window bar. I try not to breathe too quickly. I don't want to sweat. I raise my eyes and look at the building opposite: LifeStar Corporation's Head Office. A vast modern building stretching to the sky, the windows and tiles are coated so it shines silver in the light. The multinational has convinced the world it's working for a sustainable future, that it's at the cutting edge of climate restitution research. I count up twenty-seven floors. Dad's office will still be there with its bookshelves and floor-to-ceiling window. He liked watching the sunset over London. He had pictures of us on his desk; we only went inside once, and I spun round fast in his chair.

I wonder who's doing Dad's job now? And will they, like my father, ever feel compelled to tell the truth about LifeStar's relationship with the military? About their involvement in the creation of a weapon of mass destruction? I'd like to think they will, that their conscience will burn a hole in their loyalty to that company. But I know they won't. They'll have seen what happened to Dad. It would stop anyone in their tracks. I finish my drink and leave.

A voice intrudes on my thoughts. 'This coffee isn't hot enough.'

'Sorry?' I say.

'I'd like another one, but the milk needs to be hotter.'

I'm staring at a young woman with long dark hair and dark eyes. She reminds me of my last girlfriend, Mary, only Mary never dressed like she worked in an office. I remake her coffee and watch her walk out. From behind, walking away, she's even more like Mary. I don't get it, how I keep seeing people who remind me of Mary.

Ollie sidles over humming some tune. He's oozing happiness and must really be in love. And then suddenly it hits me, a physical pain, almost a punch in the stomach, how much I miss Mary. It's three months since we broke up and the hurt's not got better; I don't get that either. I keep thinking I'm alright, that I've got over her, and then I discover I'm not.

Neither of us officially ended it, but Mary went back to Scotland.

'I love you, Dom,' she cried, 'but I hate London. I want to go home.'

I've had three months of no sex and no one to confide in. That's what gets me because if she were here I'd be able to tell her about Dad. She'd understand why I want to see him. She'd take my side even if Charley and Flint disagreed.

What's she doing now, back in the Highlands and working in her father's shop: stacking shelves with tins of food, making a delivery or talking to customers? I feel sick. Gregory, her father, won the war between us.

We escaped to London in Gregory's pickup truck, and

the battle started twenty-four hours later. He confronted us. I watched the tears track his cheeks as he begged her to go home with him. His hard old face crumpled in grief and I almost relented on her behalf. But Mary stayed with me and he quickly recovered. It was impossible for us to see eye to eye. He betrayed us to the Disciples when we lived in his rental cottage; they'd never have found us without him.

'What do you want, Dominic?' he'd ask. 'For me to apologise for not letting MI5 arrest you? They knew you were in the village, and you're the ones who said they'd torture you if they got you.'

Every week Gregory told Mary how much he missed her, and how the business was suffering in her absence. And London's harsh. Being deaf made it even harder for Mary (even though she can lip-read well). She struggled to find work, she struggled to fit in. I did what I could for her, I tried my best, but in the end she went back to Gregory.

I get home and look at the last thing Mary gave me. I keep it flat and safe within the cover of a hardback notebook. A golden eagle feather. It's not your usual sort of present, but Mary's not like other people. She offered me it the last night we spent together. We sat down and she told me how a part of her would always love me. She spoke softly in her distinctive voice and gave it to me.

'Remember how when my mum died, I told you I asked the eagle for some of its strength?'

I nodded but couldn't answer. She really did call on bird spirits for help. I'd laughed at her once for that, but I didn't then. I was very serious.

'Well,' she said, 'I've been thinking about it. And I want you to have this feather, because golden eagles have strength and power, and … I hope you always have those qualities when you need them.'

I couldn't reply. A part of me wanted to destroy it, to break the feather in two, to tell her I didn't care about any of that – I just wanted her to stay. But I did none of those things. Instead, I held the feather in the palm of my hand and stroked its long spine and brown filaments. It made my fingers tingle, don't ask why.

I managed to speak. 'What are you, Mary? A witch, an angel, or just some girl I met?'

She didn't reply, but her eyes filled with tears, and for a moment I thought I couldn't bear her going, I couldn't survive …

'Dom, why are you crying?'

I turn. Charley's come into my room; I didn't hear her. I close the notebook quickly, the feather safe inside. I swallow hard and wipe my cheeks. 'Just … I miss Mary.'

She watches me. 'You should go and see her,' she says softly.

'Can't.' I shake my head. 'It's been too long and …'

'You can, Dom.' She walks over and sits on the bed beside me. 'You so obviously still love her. I couldn't understand why you didn't contact her over Christmas – you were so miserable.'

I gaze at my sister. 'I didn't know you thought that.'

She shrugs. 'What could I say when it's between you and her? But I liked her as your girlfriend.'

I almost laugh, relieved. 'I … I was never really sure how you or Flint felt about her. You know, we're so close, and then she joined us.'

'We love her, Dom, but she wasn't happy in London. She left the city, but not because she stopped loving you.'

I don't know why I didn't talk about it more at the time. Sometimes Charley sees things I fail to. 'It's felt hard,' I admit, 'being apart. I just wanted it to be different, you know, like I could say, "Oh, she's just a girlfriend, I'll get over it," but …'

Charley shakes her head gently. 'I don't think the heart's that simple, Dom.' Our eyes meet. 'Go to her.'

'But there's her fucking father,' I say, angry.

'Dom, you love her, fight for her. You're not a coward.'

'No,' I say, growing calmer.

Later, I get out my phone. My hands are shaking slightly. I draft a text. No images, no acronyms, but serious like a letter. 'Mary, I'm sorry. I've made such a mistake. I love you. I want to come and see you.' Is that alright? After three months what should I say? I press send. But what if she's found somebody else? What if everything I feel now is one sided and she's moved on? The seconds of silence extend. I don't know how long I'll have to wait. But then I get an emoji back: a simple, happy smile.

CHAPTER 3

It takes a day to travel to Mary. We agree she'll pick me up at the station. I get off the train and look around. There's a shelter but little else. There are a few people on the platform but not Mary. It's cold and dark, but the snow has melted. I walk to the car park. The other passengers get in their cars and drive off. I am alone.

I wait. I'm not sure why she's late, but she'll be here soon. I glance at my phone but there's nothing. I consider texting her, but the longer I wait the more I decide not to. The possibility she might not show chills me. Maybe she liked the idea of seeing me, but the more she's thought about it she's changed her mind. I'm not good for her; she'd be justified in thinking that.

Headlights emerge through the dark. Gregory's pickup truck swerves into the car park. Mary gets down. She calls across to me.

'Sorry I'm late, I was doing a delivery, and Mrs Jameson, I couldn't shut her up, she just wouldn't let me go and …'

She's standing in front of me, her breath visible in the air.

'I love you,' I say quickly. I'm so relieved she's there.

She smiles. She's beautiful; her dark hair is longer and her face open. Her gaze is kind. 'Aye,' she says softly.

We embrace. Her warm body is against mine. We hug for a while then release each other. I wonder if I should try to kiss her. But then we both start laughing. It's strange, almost awkward, being back together. We walk to the pickup truck and sit inside a while in silence.

'I missed you.' I look directly at her so she can read my lips. 'And … I'm sorry.'

'I missed you too,' she says. 'You shouldn't have stayed away so long.' Her eyes are serious. I hurt her.

'No, you left and I … I was very upset and …' I pause. 'I realise now, I want to be with you, even if it's just for some of the time.' I've been thinking about that the whole journey. 'Nobody knows me like you do, Mary.'

She's still. 'No, they don't.'

'I hurt you, Mary. That's not right. I never wanted to hurt you. I'm sorry.'

'Yes,' she says. 'You'll have to make up for it.'

'I will. I want to.' And then I can't bear how serious everything feels. I look down, ashamed.

She whispers. 'You can kiss me if you like.'

I raise my eyes slowly; she appears shy. I lean over and gently brush my lips against hers. We exchange a few soft kisses, then I draw her closer to me and kiss her more deeply.

'I like that,' she says as we draw apart.

'Yes.' I smile. I already feel better.

Mary drives us to their grocery store. We are quiet because she has to concentrate on the road, but I fold my hand over hers as she changes gear. We stop in the parking lot at the back of the small parade of shops.

'How's your dad?' I ask.

'He's okay. He knows you're coming, he took it pretty well.'

'He did? But he hates me.'

'He doesn't hate you, Dom. He's been angry with you, but he's not so angry now.'

Before we can say any more, I get out of the truck; better to face the guy than talk about him. We go into their shop. Gregory is serving a customer, a middle-aged woman, and they're chatting away. He glances over and acknowledges my presence with a brief nod. He carries on talking; it sounds like local gossip. I follow Mary through to the back where there's a door marked 'Private'. It leads to the stairs that take us to their flat, and then I'm standing in their large open-plan living room. There's a sofa, armchair and TV. The sofa is new but nothing else has changed. The table they eat off is near the door to the kitchen. There's an old-fashioned feel to it all, clean and cosy. I let my rucksack drop to the floor.

Through the window, the evening sky is already dotted with stars. The flat is quiet. All I can hear are shuffling sounds from the shop below. Mary takes my hand and silently leads me into her room. We face each other. I don't know why but I feel nervous. I raise my hand to touch her cheek. She leans into it and then we kiss again. Our mouths open and we kiss more deeply. It's been months since we've had sex and suddenly we can't wait. Her hands move to the belt on my jeans. We're quickly half naked and falling onto her bed. She laughs and I silence her with a kiss. I think of her father downstairs then push him from my mind. I kiss her soft skin. Her legs wrap around me and I move inside her.

Afterwards, we don't stay on the bed for long. I couldn't bear for Gregory to find us. Instead, when he shuts the shop and comes upstairs, we're in the kitchen preparing dinner. He looks at me a while.

'You look well,' he says. I'm not sure if it's an innocent comment or a euphemism. I suspect he knows what we've been up to.

'Thanks,' I say as easily as I can. 'You look good too.'

'Old, Dominic. I'm getting old, too quickly, although I don't doubt I'm doing a lot better than your poor old father.'

I'm shocked. I wasn't sure he'd even mention Dad, let alone be so blunt. It takes me time to respond. 'You saw the news?'

'The whole world knows the news, Dominic.'

I feel my heart begin to race. Is it possible …?

'I'd like to see him,' I say.

'There's a fat chance of that happening,' he says, but not unkindly.

I'm finding it difficult to breathe. 'I think it might be possible, if … if I could contact the right people.'

He looks at me, unsure. Then he shakes his head and walks over to a cabinet in the living room.

'Would you like a drink? I've got a nice local whisky here. Distillery's not far away.'

'Yeah, thanks.' The subject has moved on. That might have been my only chance to talk about Dad.

Gregory pours me a large drink. He starts to hand it over then stalls. 'How old are you now?'

'Don't worry, it's legal. I'm eighteen.' He knows full well I am.

'Really? You're still a kid to me.' He passes over the glass.

We say 'Cheers' and I take a sip of whisky. It burns my throat, strong and peaty. Mary is concentrating on the cooking, and I can't judge how much of our conversation she's lip-read. Gregory moves to sit in the armchair and indicates I take the sofa. Mary puts a lid on the pan and comes to sit by me.

'Where you staying?' Gregory asks.

'Here … if that's alright with you?' I say politely, although it feels like we're playing a game.

'He's staying here, Dad,' Mary states plainly.

'I guess the sofa's comfy enough.' He gestures.

Mary shakes her head and raises her eyes to heaven. He smiles at me. I'm increasingly uncomfortable; he's so hard to deal with.

'Gregory.' I decide to be bold. I won't be a coward. 'Can we be honest with each other?'

'Please, Dominic, be honest. I'd consider it a first.' He keeps smiling.

'Okay.' I hold my voice steady. 'I love Mary, and I take it as her father, you do too. So, as we both love Mary, can we find a way of relating … of relating without the bullshit?' I can barely believe what I'm saying. He could throw me out, but I've had enough of the way he behaves towards me.

'I'd love to know you without the bullshit, Dominic. Then I might know who I'm relating to.' His eyes bore into me. 'Shall we start with what you're really doing here, apart from having sex with my daughter? What is it you really want? Do you plan on taking her away again?'

Mary's eyes are wide, she's breathing hard. She hates this but I need to have it out with him.

'I love Mary,' I tell him. 'I thought that with her coming back up here, I could stop loving her, I could make it go away, but it didn't. So I'm here to see my girlfriend. I don't intend on asking her to come back to London. She wasn't happy there, and I don't want her to be unhappy.' I stop. Finally, I've made that clear. If that's what he's worried about, he needn't be.

'I don't want you getting her pregnant or trying to get her in some other way.'

I shake my head. 'Jesus, you really are old.' I'm struggling to stay polite. 'Mary and I are both responsible people. We take precautions.'

Mary's voice is suddenly loud. 'Neither of you own me so you can both stop talking about me like you do. I love Dom, but I choose to live here, Dad. It's not because of one of you or the other, it's because that's what I want. It's my choice.'

We are quiet. She's shamed us both. I look away, embarrassed. I hate being like this.

'Why else did you come here?' Gregory eventually asks softly.

I turn my eyes slowly to him. Do I have the courage to say it? 'I want to ask you a favour,' I whisper, 'to contact the Disciples, to ask if I can see my father.' I swallow. 'You've got your daughter. I'd like to see my father, and you're the only person I know who's contacted them.' There, I've said it, but the world is slightly out of focus. I put my head in my hands and breathe deeply. I hadn't fully realised until that moment, but that's also why I'm here. I hope Mary understands. I turn my head towards her.

'I'm sorry,' I mouth, 'but I want that too.'

Her eyes are bright, her face still. 'It's okay,' she says. 'I understand.'

I sit a little straighter and allow my eyes to return to Gregory.

'I prefer it when you're honest.' He exhales. 'Then I know what I'm dealing with.'

'Will you do it?' I ask, unsure what's happening.

'I'll think about it,' he says cautiously. 'It's … not without its risks, and I need to consider if those risks are worth it.'

'Okay.' I nod. What he's said is reasonable although what I feel about it isn't.

CHAPTER 4

We eat together, a tasty meal of fish and rice that's much better than anything I've had in the house share. The atmosphere between us is more relaxed. Gregory asks about life in London and I tell him it's not great.

'You should think about moving up here,' he says casually. 'You'd have a much better time of it.'

'Yeah? And what would I do?'

'Always some kind of work to be had round here,' he says. 'I can't see that making coffees amounts to much.'

I watch him for a long moment. His big, thick-fisted hands. The determined way in which he eats.

'You had much chance to play your music?' he asks.

I wasn't expecting that. 'No,' I say slowly. 'I mean the old sax Flint helped me get … I don't know why, but I haven't played it much.'

He shakes his head. 'You'll never be a musician like that then, will you?' He glances across at Mary. 'Mary says she can pick up on the vibrations when you play. She reckons you might be quite good.'

I don't know what to say. I look down, confused. Gregory does know things about me, but he's always behaved like he doesn't give a toss. Before Dad was arrested all I wanted to do was be a musician. Is Gregory trying to shame me now for not playing, or is he genuinely interested?

I look up. 'You're right. I should play more often. I should be practising every day.'

He shrugs. 'You're the one who knows about these things, not me.'

After dinner, we watch the television a while. Some stupid sitcom that isn't very funny. Gregory tuts as though the people who made it should have known better. Then the news comes on. There's a report about the raid on Colchester House. The police are offering money for information and they rarely do that.

Detective Inspector Graham starts his statement. 'We believe that the raid on Colchester House had a high level of support from others, many of whom will be within the criminal community. We're offering twenty thousand pounds for information that leads to a significant breakthrough and arrests.'

None of us comment on the report. But I think it's good, a sign the police are struggling with the investigation. Gregory switches off the TV, puts down the remote and rises from his armchair.

'I'm off to bed.' He nods at us and walks out.

Mary and I are alone. I glance at the sofa then we both go quietly to her room.

I am back with the Disciples, swimming underwater: alone, deep down in the sea. A wetsuit clings to my body and my naked hands and face are freezing. Air bubbles from my mouth. I've no oxygen tank, no breathing apparatus, but there's a bomb strapped to my back.

I reach the oil pipeline, unstrap the bomb and prepare to attach it. I put it in place, but believe I can stop it going off. I can disobey Gil. I'll leave out the third wire because they told me without it, the bomb won't explode. Then, suddenly, I'm no longer breathing underwater; I've lost the ability to do it. Instead, the sea is flooding my lungs. I'm on the sea bed, too far down to get to the surface in time. I'm drowning, breath by breath. A dark terror engulfs me.

I wake, gasping, gulping down air. My body is covered in sweat. My eyes scramble round the room looking for something familiar. But it's not familiar. Then I sense Mary beside me. I'm in her bed. I need to calm down. It was a dream, a terrifying dream, but that's all; I've had it before. I get up slowly, throw on a T-shirt and leave her room. I take a piss then walk into the living room. Everything is in shadow although the curtains are still open. It's so dark outside it doesn't matter that the curtains are open.

A voice from the kitchen makes me jump. 'Trouble sleeping?'

'Jesus, you scared me.'

Gregory comes into the room. He's stirring a hot drink. 'Want a camomile tea?'

I shake my head. Gregory and camomile tea don't go together in my mind. 'Just … just had a bad dream,' I say.

He comes over to where I'm looking out the window. We don't talk for a while, both of us gazing into the distance.

'I've been thinking about your request,' he says in a low voice. 'I'll contact the Disciples if that's what you really want, but it's on the condition you stop seeing Mary. You'll become too dangerous. The police are hunting them down, and it's clear they're not going to stop. MI5 will be drawing on all their resources, and you'll be entering their world.'

I listen carefully.

His voice drops even more. 'I like you so I'd take the risk, but only once, and then you're gone.'

I've never heard him talk like this before. He's never said he likes me. Yet this could be his ultimate trump card for getting me away from Mary. Still, the tone of his voice is sincere. It feels an important moment. I think of Charley and Flint; they don't know what I'm doing, and they'd never approve. And my dream, that recurring dream, is full of foreboding. What should I do?

'If you were my father,' I ask Gregory carefully, 'what would you want me to do?'

A part of me knows my father would want me to stay safe. Everything he's advised us to do is about staying safe.

'I'm not your father,' Gregory says slowly, 'so I can't answer that.'

We are both very still. The choice is stark. Or maybe there isn't any choice at all?

'I love Mary,' I say firmly. 'We never spoke of the Disciples.'

'Correct.' He nods and we leave the room.

I spend the next few days with Mary. We go on a long walk together and have time on our own, and then I help her and Gregory in the shop, lugging stock around and doing an inventory. We're relaxed with each other. Gregory and I almost joke together. Mary and I spend the nights in her bed but try to keep the noise down. We're catching up on lost time. Sex always makes me feel better, and I forget for a while that I know about Dad, and there's nothing I can do for him.

On Sunday, the store is closed and Gregory suggests we all go out together. We leave after a hearty breakfast, wrap up warm and head to their favourite loch. It's where Mary and I first made love, not that Gregory knows that. We take a stash of stuff: rugs to sit on, a blanket, a flask of hot coffee, biscuits, binoculars, and a large kite.

'I love this place,' I say, gazing out over the landscape and the expanse of water before me. 'It's still the most beautiful place I've been to.'

'Well, you'll certainly not find this in London,' Gregory says.

'Here, Dad.' Mary passes him the binoculars. He puts them to his eyes and seems to settle into his own private reverie.

'Fancy flying the kite?' Mary smiles at me.

'Sure,' I say. But I've never flown a kite in my life. This

one is huge with a complicated set of pulleys and strings. I've no idea what I'm doing. Mary watches me and giggles. I try to launch it, the wind coming in brief gusts, but it all just tangles. I try again, hoping to look like I know what I'm doing, or at least like I can get out of the tangled mess I'm in. I hear Mary's sweet laughter rising. Then I trip over the kite and I'm sprawled on the ground, the offending item docile beside me. I'm like a slapstick comic act. Gregory starts laughing too.

'Oh, Dom. You're the best for trying,' Mary calls over.

'What a townie,' Gregory says. 'No idea how to fly a simple kite or understand the wind.'

They're both laughing at me, but I don't mind. 'I admit defeat. The kite's beaten me.' I roll over onto my back and crease up too.

I hear Gregory. 'Aye, but you know how to entertain us.'

Mary comes over and stands above me, smiling. 'I love you,' she mouths.

'For what?' I mouth back.

She shrugs. 'Just for being … you.'

I grab her hand and pull her down beside me. We hug and roll on the grass, her laughter ringing through the air.

Then my clothes are damp and cold. We go and sit with Gregory, share out the biscuits, and he points out the breeds of bird he can see through the binoculars. We stay there until the coffee is drunk and we are too cold to stay any longer. Driving back, I realise just how happy I am. It's been a good day.

We spend the evening together watching television. I'm aware it's my last night with Mary and the two of us grow quiet. At some point, she gets up to go into the kitchen. Gregory and I are alone.

'I'm glad you came,' he says softly, although he keeps his eyes on the TV. 'Mary … she's happier when you're around.'

'Thanks,' I say, although I feel quite choked. I never thought I'd hear him say that.

Monday morning and my trip is over. Mary, Gregory and I stand in the living room. I put my rucksack on my back and check my ticket; everything's in order. I'll weave my way to Glasgow, and then it's straight down to London.

'Thank you for having me,' I say to Gregory. 'I really appreciate it.'

He nods. 'Take care, Dominic,' he says gruffly. He puts out his hand to shake mine. I take it and then I feel it, a piece of paper in the palm of his hand. For a moment I stall. Then I wrap my fingers around it so when the handshake is over the paper can't be seen.

Mary drives me to the station. The train comes in and we say goodbye. I kiss her long and hard. Her eyes follow me as I move down the carriage to find a seat. I sign to her, 'I love you.' It's something she taught me long ago, although it's the only sign language I know.

The train pulls away. I watch her grow smaller until she's out of view. I put my head back and close my eyes. I can feel the paper in my hand. When I eventually open it, I keep my fingers curled so no one can see its message. 'Platform 7, Glasgow Central Station.' My heart skips a beat. He's done it. Gregory made contact with the Disciples. I don't fully understand why, but that probably doesn't matter. I'll meet them today. I'm going to see my father. I scrunch up the paper, pop it in my mouth, chew it and swallow.

CHAPTER 5

Platform 7, Glasgow Central. My heart is pounding. All I can see are CCTV cameras watching everything. This cannot be a good place to meet. People rush by, someone is talking loudly on their phone, and in the distance a young woman is waving at me.

'Dominic,' she calls.

I try to control my panic, I've no idea what's going on. She's wearing a long vintage coat and has a large bag over her shoulder; it's stuffed with books. She comes forward and throws her arms around me in a hug.

'We're students,' she whispers in my ear, 'play along. Follow me.' She releases her embrace and says casually, 'I hope you appreciate I've cut class to see you.'

My mouth is dry. I need to improvise. 'Yeah, well, sorry I took so long. And … how's …'

'McKenzie?' She smiles. 'Getting over his hangover, but he'll be pleased to see you.'

We leave the station and its cameras. We discuss a recent movie, one at least I've seen, and keep walking.

'We won't bother with the bus,' she says, 'despite the weather.' Okay, that's good, we'll avoid the cameras there too.

We walk for some time and walking helps me relax. We get to a stylish old block of flats. She presses number 12. The front door opens and we slip inside. Panic returns. We walk up two flights of stairs and the flat's door is ajar. She indicates I go ahead and I step inside.

The barrel of a gun greets me. I'm back with the Disciples. Bile rises in my throat as the door closes behind me; the woman who met me disappears. The man holding the gun is like the Disciples I've known before. He's older than me, probably in his twenties, and tough. Longish hair, tattoos on his arms, pierced ears and nose. And the look in his eyes is hard and unrelenting. He draws his fingers across his lips instructing me to stay silent.

'Take off your clothes,' he says slowly.

'What?' I mumble. He glares at me for speaking.

'I don't know if you're wired, so you're going to take off your clothes, and then I'll know.'

The gun doesn't move. Do they really imagine I'm wired? That the police or MI5 sent me? I take off my jacket, hoodie and T-shirt, then undo my jeans.

'All of them,' he says. I'm standing in my underwear.

I consider refusing; he's humiliating me.

'All of them,' he repeats, losing patience.

I don't argue. I strip naked. He walks over and circles me slowly. He insists I raise my arms and spread my legs. I try not to meet his eyes. He kicks my clothes away and then goes through them. He removes my phone from the jacket pocket, opens it and takes out the SIM. After checking everything he stands back.

'Okay, you can get dressed now.'

I put on my clothes and he tells me to sit in the living room. There are two sofas, both of them covered with Indian-style throws. Bookshelves are stacked with academic texts. I notice dirty plates, a tea-stained mug and the distinct smell of essential oils. I've only known one Disciples hideout – a massive mansion on acres of land in the Highlands. It was the antithesis of this.

'Hello, Dominic.' It's a woman's voice, familiar. I turn to see Gemma in the doorway.

'Hey,' I say, standing. I can't help smiling, relieved I know her. Gemma was the one Disciple who showed me true kindness.

'Stay seated,' she says and comes to sit beside me. I don't know how she can look beautiful, living with the Disciples, but she does. There is something about her long hair and green eyes I've always liked. And of course, she was Gil's girlfriend. Not that the Disciples ever admit to anything as possessive as girlfriends or boyfriends.

'Your father's not great,' she says, serious. 'We've had a doctor check him over, and got him medication for his blood pressure and heart.'

I'm silent, shocked. My father never took medication for anything. He was a strong and healthy man.

'But psychologically, the problem's worse.'

I listen, trying to take it in. 'What do you mean "psychologically"?'

'He's mute.'

'What?'

'He's mute. We don't think he can't speak, rather that he's just not. It's a response to trauma. Probably … it was his way of closing down. Holding back as much as he could.'

My lower lip starts to tremble. 'Are you saying he … he's not speaking at all?'

She nods. 'Gil is prepared to let you see him because he thinks your presence may help. We know he's got a lot of in-formation to share, to tell us, but we can't unlock it. Perhaps you can. We owe it to your father to allow that possibility. The choice, however, is yours.'

I feel light-headed. We're quiet for a while.

'Is he here?' I ask.

'No. We've got a journey to get to him. This flat we're … borrowing. When we leave, we'll put the key back under the doormat.'

The air feels hard to breathe. The smell of essential oils is cloying.

'We don't have a lot of time. You either come now or continue on your journey home.'

I feel sick. I think of Charley and Flint. I should get out now or they might never forgive me. This is too risky; I might disappear into the Disciples' world for good. 'If I come with you,' I ask carefully, 'will I be able to go home afterwards?'

'Of course. This is about your father, Dominic, not you.'

I hope she's telling the truth. 'Then I'd like to see him.'

Gemma nods. 'This is what's going to happen. He's in a safe house and you can't know where.' She withdraws a small tin from her pocket and opens it. I'm staring at two tablets. 'You're going to take these then we'll walk downstairs and get into a car. Riley and I will sit in the front, you'll lie down on the floor in the back. We'll put some rugs over you so you can't be seen. The tablets will put you to sleep and when you wake up we'll be there.'

I'll be losing all control. I won't even be conscious.

'It's for your own safety, ours and your father's,' Gemma insists.

I swallow hard. Did I ever imagine this would be easy? No, I didn't think it through at all.

I finally nod and stretch out my hand for the tablets.

CHAPTER 6

I wake, groggy, lying on my side. My eyes slowly focus on a table. A rickety wooden table and chairs. Someone is sitting there. Riley, that's his name. He pointed a gun at me, he told me to strip. The gun is on the table now. And then I remember – Dad. He's here, somewhere.

I sit up awkwardly. My limbs aren't functioning properly, it's like I'm drunk.

'You're awake.' Riley looks over.

'Just … just feel very woozy.'

'It'll wear off,' he says, without concern. 'Hungry?'

I shake my head. Still, he gets up and pours me a glass of water. 'This should help.' He passes it to me.

I take in my surroundings. Sparse and simple like some basic country kitchen. The bench I'm sitting on is hard. The blinds on the windows are down.

'Where are we? England or Scotland?' I ask.

'It doesn't matter.'

The kitchen is cold, and outside I bet there are fields surrounding us. We're in the middle of nowhere. I gulp down the water and my head starts to clear.

'Can I see my father?'

'Gemma suggested you wait until she comes back. She's been looking after him.'

Somehow, that's comforting.

'He's sleeping,' Riley says.

I look at my watch, it's seven in the evening. I've been out for hours. I get up and walk round the kitchen stretching my legs. Behind the blinds, it's dark. A shuffling sound comes from the hallway. I turn to Riley and his eyes meet mine. 'Sounds like he's up.'

I watch the doorway. The old man who appears is not familiar. His beard and moustache are almost white, and he's lost most of his hair. His eyes fall on Riley; they appear full of mist – he's confused. Slowly, he turns to look at me, a terrifying, vacant stare. He's not my father, and yet he is. I stop breathing. I can't find my voice and my mouth tastes of grit. I've wanted this moment for so long, I've imagined it many times, but not like this.

'Dad,' I whisper.

He stares at me. He's smaller, like his frame has shrunk.

'Dad.' I struggle. Riley looks on.

I try to speak more clearly. 'Dad, it's me. Dominic.' Then after a few deep breaths, I say, 'Your son.'

His face softens. His eyes fill. His lips move but no sound comes out. His expression clouds with anguish. He starts to tremble and I can see him struggling. Struggling to get something out from deep inside.

'Dom … in … ic.' It isn't his voice, not as I've ever heard it, but a distorted growl. His lips keep moving, but the sound takes a while.

'Dom … in … ic.' This time he's louder, but it's haunting.

'Dominic!' he wails.

He coughs, choking. I should go to him but I can't move. Gradually, his coughing lessens.

'Dominic,' he whispers; his throat sounds sore. 'My son.'

I nod. Finally I manage to hug him, his small, thin body. He used to feel strong and protective. But now I can't speak, a hug is the only language I have. I hold him close, my body shaking slightly. I feel his arms rise to hug me. I'm crying. This is my father now: we lost so much and we'll never get it back.

'Dominic. You're alive.' He hugs me tighter. He isn't as weak as he looks.

'Dad.'

After a while, he pulls away from me. He stands back to take me in. 'My son.'

'I'm here.' I wipe the tears from my cheeks.

But the colour starts to drain from his face. He's exhausted. He turns and walks away. I follow him to his bedroom. His room is also sparse and bare: a bed, a chest of drawers, and a wooden chair. He lies down and closes his eyes. I sit on the chair at the side of his bed.

He rests for a while, and then, without opening his eyes, he says quietly, 'They almost killed me. I don't know how I survived.' He pauses, speaking is an effort. 'My body wouldn't give out, and … there was no means to end it.' He breathes a few long, laboured breaths. 'They don't allow suicide, they just kill you slowly.'

I don't want to hear this, yet it's his truth.

'But … I stayed silent.' He exhales. 'I stopped talking. They don't know everything.'

I swallow hard. 'You're stronger than you think.'

His eyes flutter behind his closed eyelids. 'I'm very tired,' he says weakly. 'Talk to me, Dominic. I … I'd just like to hear your voice.'

Whenever I've imagined speaking to him again, I've always thought I'd tell him what the Disciples did to us. I'd shout in anger, and rage about how his choices hurt us. But I don't do that. It won't help anything. Instead, I tell him things as though everything is alright. I speak softly. Charley and I are well. So is Rena, his sister; she looked after us with care and kindness. We don't see her much, but still, she's there in the background. And we're close to Flint, Rena's son, Charley in particular. I pause, waiting to see if there is any response. He is silent but I think he's still awake.

'They're kind of an item,' I say carefully, 'but that's okay, because although they're cousins Flint's adopted, and he's completely different to what he was like when he was a child.' I'm trying to justify Flint because my father doesn't know him now. He'd looked down on Rena and the way she brought up her son. 'He's one of the best people I think I'll ever know.'

Again, I watch his face for some kind of reaction. Perhaps he's dropped off? It's been a long time since I've seen the contour of his face, his distinctive features, the rise and fall of his chest. Once, as a child, I walked into his bedroom and found him asleep; it was a Sunday afternoon and he'd been working late all week. I noted all the ways we were physically alike and different. He looked peaceful then, but less so now. I stand up slowly to leave.

'Don't go,' he whispers, 'I can still hear you.'

I sit again. But what should I say? I tell him about Mary, and how special I think she is. 'I hope that when you meet her you like her.'

Before Dad was arrested, I'd never have gone out with someone like Mary. She just wouldn't have been on my radar; I cared too much about what people thought of me. 'Yeah, Dad, I hope you like her.'

He listens but doesn't say anything. At some point, he snores. I feel tired too. I walk to the door.

I hear his voice behind me. 'There are people who love you.'

I turn. 'Yes, Dad. There are people who love me.'

He smiles then shifts onto his side and is quickly asleep.

'Are you okay?' Gemma asks. She's waiting in the kitchen; I didn't hear her arrive. Riley is sitting reading a book.

'I think I'm okay,' I say coolly, although I'm not sure.

She indicates we leave the kitchen and takes me into the bedroom off it. There are two single beds; only one has been slept in. She closes the door behind us and leaves the light off. I'm glad for the dark.

'It's been a big day for you,' she says gently.

'Yes,' I say, but my voice shakes slightly.

'It's okay if you cry, just not in front of him. You, we, don't want to upset him. Keep the topics of conversation light. There are things he doesn't need to know.'

She doesn't want me telling him about what happened with them, of course not. 'I already know that, Gemma.'

She nods. She watches me closely through the hazy darkness. 'I always think of you with affection, Dominic,' she says softly. 'We missed you after you went.'

I have no idea how to respond. We left because we had to. Gil almost shot me in the process. Yet she sounds genuine.

'I remember you as kind, Gemma. And … I'm glad it's been you who's been looking after Dad. I think you're the best Disciple to be doing that.'

'That was Gil's decision,' she says matter-of-factly. 'As he put it, "a personal request". I'm not as involved in direct action at the moment.'

'Okay.'

Then she says quietly, 'I'm a mother now, and that changes things a bit.'

'Wow.' I'm shocked.

'The timing isn't great, but I couldn't refuse Gil's request.' She half smiles.

'Is he … the father of your child?'

She doesn't reply. But suddenly I see it quite clearly, a picture in my head of her child.

'You have a son and he looks like Gil.'

Her voice sharpens. 'Dominic, I have more than one lover and so does he. This topic of conversation is closed.' She's agitated. She's said too much; it's none of my business and a security risk. I need to change the subject.

'Do you know what they have planned for Dad?' I ask.

'We would like you to stay for a few days until he's ready to speak to Gil.'

'Of course.' I nod. 'I want to stay with him.'

'Longer term …' She shrugs. 'There are various possibilities.'

'Charley, can Charley see him? I think she'd want to see Dad too.'

'You approached us, Dominic. Not her. We recognise … Charley's animosity to the Disciples. I'm sure at some point she'll see him, but not now.'

I'm quiet. I'm not here because of their kindness. They want something from me, and I will provide it. I've seen my father but they're in complete control.

CHAPTER 7

I spend the following days with Dad. The cottage is an enclosed world, a quiet place where we can talk. Riley is a constant presence, and Gemma joins us briefly each evening. I sleep in the bedroom with Riley but I don't sleep well. I know Charley should be here too, that Dad would love to see her. I also know she and Flint will be as mad as hell with me: I'm back with the Disciples. They will have contacted Mary when I didn't return. And I hope they've phoned Magda and made up some excuse to explain my absence. I don't want to lose my job.

As my time with Dad is limited, I make the most of what I've got. At first, he says very little. I'm amazed at how much I can say without telling him about what happened to us. I chat about the home we lived in, the things we used to do together, and how we'll hopefully be able to do them again some time. He listens and nods occasionally. He even manages to smile. But I can see he's also tired; something in him has drained away.

'Did the Disciples look after you?' he eventually asks.

'Yes,' I lie, and he doesn't ask any more.

He gradually comes back to himself. We can't go outside, but I notice he's increasingly aware of his surroundings. He comments on a book Riley is reading, and on the winter light seeping in behind the blinds. He even dares to look in the mirror.

'I don't recognise myself,' he says, 'I don't know when I got so old.'

'You're not that old, Dad.' I want him to know he's got lots of life left. I stand beside him, both our reflections in the bathroom mirror.

He smiles. 'You haven't changed much, Dom.'

'You used to say I looked like you when you were young.' We've got the same blue eyes and, before it turned grey, he also had mousy-coloured hair. 'Genes, you said.'

'Genes,' he repeats.

And I almost ask him the question that has etched itself into my thoughts: why did he give us the ability to breathe underwater? Why that genetic mutation? But I don't, because he grows very serious and his expression changes as though a shadow has darkened the back of his mind.

It is evening, Saturday. I've been with Dad for five full days and he's definitely getting stronger. The four of us sit down to eat. He finishes first, wipes his mouth then looks at me quizzically.

'Dominic, you haven't mentioned your music.'

He loved my playing and took pride in what a good musician I was. He spent a lot of money on my lessons and instruments.

'No, I …' I hesitate. 'After you went, I found it hard to play.'

He watches me. 'But, Dom, you're a musician. Musicians don't stop playing.'

'I think sometimes they do, Dad, if … if …' I stall. 'If the music inside them stops.'

'No.' He shakes his head. 'You told me very clearly, when you argued that you weren't going to do all those science exams. "I'm a musician," you said. "Don't try to make me what I'm not." You can't stop playing.'

'I did my best, Dad, but … I just couldn't. The desire left me.'

'Desire?' he says loudly. 'Desire? Life isn't about desire, Dom. It's about being the best you can be, it's about fulfilling your potential. Sometimes, you've got to go against what you feel.'

I sit there and can't believe how angry he is with me. Not Dad, not after everything.

'Do you think I "desired" whistle-blowing on LifeStar Corporation?' he shouts. 'I didn't desire it, Dominic, but it's what I had to do. You've let yourself down.'

I stare at him, stunned, but he just shakes his head again, dismissive.

Something snaps. 'Don't be disappointed in me, Dad. I stopped playing because where there used to be music inside me there was just a great big hole.' I'm shouting too. 'An empty hole and it wasn't there when you were around to be my father!'

Riley and Gemma watch me, cool and detached. My father looks distraught. How has this happened? I just wanted to see him – I thought he loved me. This place is suffocating. I glance at the front door then run for it. But Riley gets there first.

'You can't leave.'

I try to push past him and we're struggling with each other. I don't know how he does it, but he flings me into the adjacent bedroom and throws me towards my bed. My shin crashes into the metal bed frame and I yelp in pain. Then I'm flat on my face, his hand pushing my head into the mattress. I can barely breathe.

'You stay in here and shut the fuck up,' he hisses.

He lets me go. I hear the door slam shut. I lie there and I try not to think. Shame floods me. I never wanted anyone to hear me say those things. I don't want to be like this.

Later, the door opens. I don't rise to see who it is; my face is buried in the bed.

'You've upset your father.' It's Gemma. 'That's not what any of us want.'

I don't answer.

'You're not here, Dominic, to play happy families. You're here because your father has a lot of important information he needs to share with us. You've helped him find his voice. We thank you for that, but now he's asked to speak to Gil. We'll be taking you back.'

I roll over and sit up.

She hasn't finished. 'We took a significant risk bringing you here, although I recognise you don't appreciate that. You will not raise your voice again, and you don't leave without us.'

I look at her standing tall and stern in the doorway.

'When Gil gets here, the risk will increase. Nothing would please MI5 more than finding Gil and your father together. *They are after us,*' she stresses, 'and they're determined. We cannot afford to slip up or draw attention to ourselves.'

I watch her closely. 'You're afraid?'

'You should be too. Now go and make peace with your father. Once you leave here, we cannot say when you'll see him again.'

I find Dad sitting on his bed, staring at the doorway.

'I'm sorry,' I say, walking into the room. I sit near him. 'I'm sorry, Dad, that I wasn't able to be what you wanted of me. I didn't ... I never wanted to disappoint you.'

'You've not disappointed me,' he says softly. 'You're a good boy, Dom. I can see that. I'm the one who's sorry. I think ... I'd hoped that, somehow, you wouldn't suffer too much as a result of my actions, but of course you have. I've just not wanted to see it or take responsibility for, as you put it, the hole you've felt inside.'

'I missed you, Dad.'

'Yes.'

'We were only sixteen. I know you wanted me to be a man, but I couldn't stop missing you.'

'I understand.'

I cry. I want him to tell me he loves me, it's all I want to hear. He draws me to him and kisses my head. He hugs me. I cry like some stupid child and I can't stop. Eventually, I grow calmer.

'I've asked to speak to Gil,' he whispers in my ear. 'It's important now to seek justice for your suffering and mine.'

I pull away from him. 'Yes.' I sit back on the chair. We have limited time but there is something I have to talk about. I drop my voice to a whisper.

'We found your code word: Kingfisher.'

'Kingfisher?' He looks surprised.

'Yes, remember, you left it behind the seam of Charley's toy rabbit.'

I watch his eyes, but they cloud; he's struggling to remember.

'It took me, us, a long time to figure it out,' I continue, because he *must* remember. 'But in the end, I think we did.'

'Dominic, I can't recall much from that time, not when they arrested me.'

'No, Dad. It was very important and I need you to confirm we got it right. It was your way of telling us …'

He puts a finger to his lips. I stop. 'If I did leave you something,' he whispers, 'and you worked it out … then you worked it out.'

I realise he doesn't remember, and he doesn't want to lie. I'm quiet.

'I love you, Dom. You and your sister are the best things in my life.'

I listen.

'I love you,' he says gently. 'Thank you for coming. I have listened to everything you've said, and the thing that comforts me most is knowing that in your life there are people who love you. Despite everything I've done, you have people in your life who love you.'

I can't speak. I just nod, yes.

'Then that's enough.'

CHAPTER 8

I wake. The room is dark. Riley is sleeping in the bed opposite, yet I distinctly heard something. I glance through the open doorway; someone is in the kitchen. I rise slowly and walk over, my bare feet silent on the tiles. He stands by the table, a tall figure, his back towards me. He removes a gun from his jacket, opens the barrel, checks it then puts it on the table. His long hair falls forward around his face. I stand there, silent.

'Hello, Dominic.' He doesn't turn.

I draw closer. 'Gil.'

Our eyes meet. He smiles. 'It's been a while, hasn't it?' He motions to a chair and we sit opposite each other.

Nothing about him has changed. Not his dark eyes, long dark hair, pale skin or his penetrating gaze. I've hoped he'd acquire a scar or some physical marking that betrays him for what he really is, but no such thing has happened. Instead, he still looks like Jesus, the Jesus I've seen in museum pictures and books, only he's clean-shaven. And even in the darkness, his eyes are looking right through me; I hate how he does that. He sits still and calm, but I feel the power in his presence.

'You've done a good job,' he says softly. 'Your father's much improved.'

I don't answer, it's not a job.

'Are you well?'

I nod, but still can't speak.

'I knew you'd come back,' he says with ease.

I swallow hard. 'Did you?'

'Yes, when we freed your father.' He leans over and whispers. 'That's why I let you go, Dominic.'

My tongue feels numb. I know the truth; he let me go because he couldn't shoot me.

Eventually, I manage to speak. 'The raid on Colchester House was impressive.'

'Yes. It wasn't easy. We didn't think we'd be able to release your father, but luck was on our side.'

'What happens now?' I ask.

'First, I need to speak to your father, to hear all he has to say. Then … there will be important operational decisions I'll have to make.'

I want to ask him about those decisions but he wouldn't answer.

'Your father's work with us is unfinished. It needs to be brought to fruition. Justice will be done.'

'Justice,' I repeat.

He nods.

'Can I stay a while longer?'

'Why? Do you care for justice more now?'

'I might.'

He shakes his head. 'You made your position quite clear when you left us, Dominic. And you committed, as you put it yourself, an act of treachery. You're a young man who wants to stay with his father, but that isn't what we want at all.'

'I'm a young man you made a Disciple,' I retort. 'It didn't matter what I wanted. It's what you did.'

He keeps his eyes on me. 'Is that so?'

'Yes. Do you think I just walked away and forgot what happened? I live with it every single day. I think of you, Gil, every single day.' I stop. I should never have said that, not about him.

'Actually, Dominic,' he says very slowly, 'I take more responsibility for you than you realise.'

'Do you? I don't think so.'

'I know where you're living,' he says decisively. 'That you've been there for the last five months with Charley and Flint. That you make coffees in the City of London during the week, and you still, on occasion, see your girlfriend, Mary.'

'That just proves Riley's been listening to everything I've said.'

'Your landlord demands you pay him in cash,' he says, his voice hardening. 'He only declares half his earnings, and he puts it through a company he owns called Green Tree Rentals. The benign-sounding name is in direct contrast to his violation of building and safety regulations, but the poverty of those who rent from him means they've no power of recourse. You're in his best property.' His words spark with political passion; he's not changed. But how does Gil know that? He's done his research. 'I did tell you I promised your father I would do what I could to protect you.'

'Except you almost killed me twice.'

'You're still alive, and you're still relatively safe.'

I can't win this kind of argument with Gil. He's always right. 'I'm tired.'

'Then I suggest,' he says, motioning to the bedroom behind me, 'that you go back to sleep.'

I look at him and rise slowly. So this was how we met again. I turn and walk away.

The next morning, Gil goes into my father's room and they talk for hours. I don't get to see the moment they meet or the look in my father's eyes. If I did I might understand, in some way, why he involved himself with the Disciples. But except for the murmur of voices coming from his room, I hear and know nothing. I eat breakfast then crash out on my bed again. There is nothing else to do.

A phone goes off and wakes me. I haven't heard a phone for days. They told me they don't receive calls here, nothing that might be traced. I rise quickly from my bed. Is something wrong? I go into the kitchen where Riley watches Gemma closely.

'Shit,' she says; it's her phone. 'It's Margaret.' She walks past me and closes the bedroom door. She lowers her voice but we can hear everything she says. 'A temperature? How high? Has he eaten? I left milk for him in the fridge ... no, not formula milk, *my* milk ... okay, yes, I'm coming.'

She returns to the kitchen, her body tense, her expression anxious. Then I notice Gil standing at the end of the hallway. He looks at Gemma and they exchange some private message through their eyes. He nods and indicates she should go. She leaves quickly without saying goodbye. Gil turns from us and walks back into my father's room. Riley picks up his book. It's then I realise for sure that Gemma's child is Gil's. It's just over a year since I last saw her so her baby must be very young. I can't think what kind of life a child of Gil's might lead. I wouldn't want him as my father.

We all eat lunch together but Dad's distracted. His thoughts are miles away. He'd get like this sometimes at home when he was mulling over something from work. I used to hate it then and I don't like it now, but I say nothing; I won't appear a child again.

Later in the afternoon, Dad sleeps. He's exhausted and Gil says they'll speak again in the morning. Riley goes to have a bath. Gil and I are alone in the kitchen. He is thoughtful, serious. This time he sits next to me and speaks in a hushed voice.

'When Riley returns, he'll take you home. If your father's still sleeping, you leave anyway.'

I listen and realise I may not get to say goodbye to Dad. A pit starts opening in my stomach. I'm not ready to leave him.

'Your father knows … you've both said the most important things you need to.'

I'm definitely not going to be able to say goodbye. I feel quite sick.

'Go home, Dominic, and get on with the rest of your small, ordinary life.'

'My small, ordinary life?'

'Yes. Make coffees, fuck your girlfriend, play your music, and disappear into the general mass of society.'

'And what … what if I don't want to?'

'You need to for your own safety.'

I look at him. He thinks he can tell me how to live. And I don't get to say goodbye to Dad. 'No.' I shake my head. 'I'm not going. I refuse.'

He pauses. He's quite calm, which doesn't seem right either.

'I'm a Disciple, Gil. You've got to live with that.'

'It's because you're a Disciple, Dominic,' he says smoothly, 'that I'm commanding you to go home and get on with your small, ordinary life.'

'I disobey,' I say, although I know defying Gil is dangerous. Still, he isn't riled in any way.

'No.' He sighs as though I'm a small child. 'If I have to discipline you, it will be very unpleasant, not to mention deeply upsetting for your father. You don't disobey.'

I know he's won, but I can't stop. 'Don't I have a right to be involved in seeking justice for my father? A right to be involved in holding LifeStar Corporation to account and bringing it down?' I shouldn't be saying any of this; it sounds like I want to actively join them.

'You might have that right, Dominic, when I know I can trust you.' He smiles. 'Rule number one: obey your commanding officer. Disciples are disciplined. I've given you an order. Obey it.' I feel his eyes pierce my skin. 'It's what your father wants. Is that understood?'

I realise I'm going home. I have no idea when I'll see Dad again.

'Yes,' I whisper. 'I understand.'

CHAPTER 9

I'm drugged and bundled into the back of a car. Riley drives. At some point we reach a service station and then I'm in the back of a van. I sleep for a long time. Later, someone is helping me walk but I'm dazed. I sense we're back in London. Then I'm lying on a cold, hard surface, and feel the scratch of a pen on the palm of my hand. I'm quickly asleep again.

I wake, freezing. The sun is slowly rising. I'm on a park bench in a square near the house share. My body aches; I'm cold and scrunched up. I feel terrible. I think I might vomit and there's no way I can walk home. Gradually, I remember my phone. I find it in my pocket and ring Flint.

'What the fuck have you done?' His voice is loud on the other end. 'You don't ask us, you say nothing, you do what you want – forget the fucking danger …?' He goes on.

I hate him being angry with me, but he's got a right to rant. I listen until he's finished. 'I'm on a park bench across the road,' I say slowly. 'You need to come and get me, I've trouble walking.'

By the time he reaches me, Flint is calmer. I sit up on the bench and he lowers himself beside me. I want to speak but it's difficult.

'It's okay,' I eventually say. 'I saw Dad. They let me go. I'll probably never see them again.' He needs to know Gil has no hold over me; I haven't gone back to the Disciples. 'They drugged me so I didn't even know where we were. So it's finished. We're safe.'

47

He is quiet then lets out a long sigh. 'Yeah, well, you're gonna have to deal with Charley. *She is upset,*' he stresses.

'I wanted her to see Dad too, I asked them if she could, but … I couldn't get that for her.'

'Well, she's mad with you, Dom. And that you didn't tell us – she had to find out from Mary.' He shakes his head. 'I've had to listen to her for days. And I can see it her way, 'cause her whole life she's been second best with your dad, and this just proves it.'

'No, Flint, it's not that simple.' Yet I know it's also the truth. At key moments my father's been with me and not her, like when he told me he was going to whistle-blow on LifeStar.

'You can say that to me, Dom, but it ain't gonna make her feel any better.'

I lean back on the bench. I'm going to have to face the wrath of my sister. 'Oh, shit.'

'Yeah.' He sighs.

We don't walk back immediately. I can't face Charley when the others are around. I'll meet her after work and we can go for a walk … find somewhere private to talk. Flint pulls Rizla paper and a tin of tobacco out of his pocket. I watch the quiet ritual as he rolls his cigarette. He lights it and takes a long drag. It smells different for some reason. He passes it over. I don't smoke but take it anyway. I draw on it briefly then pass it back. We don't say any more.

The house is quiet when I enter it. Flint told everyone I'd gone off for a few days – a bit of time out. I sleep for a while then consider a shower, and notice the ink on the palm of my hand. An eleven-digit mobile number followed by the words: 'Emergency only. Use new SIM – discard after.' If nothing else, Gil has given me a way to contact them. I write the number in the notebook where I keep Mary's feather, just the number and nothing else. Then I shower and wash the ink off. I phone Magda. At least Charley's helped me there; she told them I was sick. I assure Magda I'm feeling a lot better, I'll be in tomorrow. I go and buy some food then head off to meet my sister.

I reach the converted old warehouse where she works, which is now an ultra-modern office block. Her job's a bit of a fluke in an up-and-coming advertising company, and it's a far cry from the medical school she'd hoped to go to. I walk into the reception area.

'Hi,' I say to the woman behind the desk. 'I'm here to see Sophie Bletchley. Can you let her know Luke Giddens is waiting when she's finished?' I figure letting her know I'm here is the best approach. She won't make a scene. The woman rings through.

'She's asked if you can go up. She's on the third floor.'

I take the lift. I've never been to her office before, and walk slowly down the corridor. It's lined with several studio rooms. I reach the last one and the door is open. I can see my sister peering at a screen. Her boss, at least I presume it's him, is standing next to her. I didn't expect him to be so young and trendy, although Charley said he was good looking. 'Not too good looking?' Flint had teased.

'Come in,' he says, barely glancing at me.

I walk over, carefully stepping around the very expensive equipment.

'What do you think?' my sister asks without looking at me.

'*I'm sorry,*' I whisper quickly into her head. Then I glance at the screen – they're looking at a set of photos.

'Wow,' I say, shocked. They're pictures of my sister. She looks quite altered. She's always been pretty but not like this: glamourous and sultry.

'I was just helping Jackson out,' she says. 'They won't be used for anything.'

Jackson raises his eyes to mine. 'I take it you're impressed.'

'I'm impressed,' I say, although something about Jackson makes me uneasy. He looks directly into my eyes for just a little too long.

'How strange,' he says. 'You have the same colour and shape of eyes as your friend.'

I glance over at Charley and shrug. 'Can't say it's something I've ever noticed.'

'Jackson has this theory,' Charley says quickly, 'that friends generally pick friends that look similar to them.'

'It's a rather narcissistic characteristic of human beings,' he says. 'We enjoy being with people like ourselves.'

'Maybe.' I shrug again. We need to get out of here.

'So where are you off to tonight?' he asks Charley as he switches off the screen.

'That's Luke's secret,' she says pleasantly, but barely looks at me. She's angry.

'Well, have fun.' Jackson smiles.

'Thanks. I'll see you tomorrow. And can I … can I have a print out of that second one?' she asks softly. 'I really like it.'

He nods.

We leave the studio and walk down the corridor.

'*I'm very angry with you, Dom,*' she says into my head. '*You have no idea.*'

'*I think I do. Let's just get outside.*'

We walk into the nearest square. No one is sitting on the park benches and the grass looks bare. The only people there are walking through it on their way home. My sister is practically marching; she's going so fast, belligerent.

'Charley, stop.' I touch her arm to slow her down. 'Please. I saw Dad and I'd like to talk to you about it, but I know you can't hear me when you're this mad.'

She turns to me. We're silent, facing each other. Her eyes fill, sad and angry. Then her hand rises quickly and she slaps me hard across the face. She's never hit me before, but I feel her rage. I'm shaking.

'Don't do that again,' I mutter.

She bursts into tears. The tension between us breaks. We're standing in the middle of the square. It's a cold winter evening and my sister's sobbing. I move to hug her.

'Why is it, Dom, that Dad's always there for you? Somehow, however it happens, he's there and you're there, but I'm left out.'

'I wanted you to be with us, but I couldn't make them do it.'

She shakes her head against me. 'You don't listen to anyone but yourself, Dom,' she mumbles into my body. 'You never stop to think about how what you do might affect me, or Flint or even Mary. She said you spent a really good weekend together but you still went off to those bastards. As if they haven't done enough harm. As if you can't stay away from them …' She hiccups, upset. 'You should never have seen Dad without me. That wasn't fair or right.'

I listen to her. I don't say anything back, it won't help. I got to see Dad but she didn't because she'd never speak to the Disciples. I hug her tighter.

'He loved hearing about you, Charley,' I whisper. 'About what you're doing, and Flint, and that we're all close and care for each other and …' She grows a little calmer. 'He knows he's hurt you but he does love you. Even though you weren't there, he still loves you so much. You're his daughter.'

Gradually, she pulls away from me. 'I just feel shit about it.' Her eyes are still glassy with tears. 'Was Gil there?' she asks. We're in a public space; she'd have been better not mentioning his name.

I nod.

'I don't ever want to see his evil face again.'

'I know. So it was me who had to see Dad.'

'Or you could have stayed away.' Her eyes meet mine but she isn't so angry now. 'How could you bear him, Dom? After everything.'

'I didn't have to. He was only there at the very end, and he was only interested in Dad, not me.'

'I have trouble believing that.'

'Really, Charley. He was quite clear. He wanted nothing to do with me. I was to go home and get on with my "small, ordinary life".'

'Your small, ordinary life?'

'That's how he put it.'

She laughs. I'm not sure why. 'I guess we must have pissed him off when we left.'

'I think so.'

She seems happier with that. 'Are you alright?'

'Yeah.'

'He didn't fill you with his shit about freedom and justice and what they can do and why you should join them?'

'He didn't even mention those words. He just wanted to talk to Dad.'

'Will he let you see Dad again?' she asks carefully.

'I don't know, Charley. I've no idea how that might happen. Like I've no idea where they're holding him. They drugged me to hide the location.'

We're both quiet. I'm aware of how sad I feel.

Charley asks, 'And you've no way of contacting them now, except through Gregory?'

'No. Gregory did me a one-off favour. It won't happen like that again. And I've no number or forwarding address.'

She seems relieved. I tell myself it's worth the lie.

'Now, shall I tell you about Dad?'

'When we get home. Flint should hear it too.'

CHAPTER 10

I tell Charley and Flint about my time with Dad. About Gemma and Riley, but little about Gil; I probably said too much to him and they don't need to know that. They visibly relax, aware I'm safe. Our time with the Disciples is truly over. Flint, in particular, laughs at the small, ordinary lives we're meant to lead. I go into work the next day, and life continues as usual.

As the weeks pass, my six days with Dad feel increasingly unreal. It's like I walked into a time warp, entered another universe, and met Dad and Gil there. Then I slipped out of it and its doors closed behind me. I watch the news regularly, but the raid on Colchester House is no longer mentioned. I wonder what information Dad has given Gil, and when he'll act on it. Maybe I'll have to wait months before hearing of some attack or release of documents?

One evening, Charley and I are walking home from the cinema. Flint's at work and we're alone. I share my thoughts with her.

'I keep having these ideas about Dad.'

'How d'you mean?' she asks.

'Just about … what might happen when his *work* with them is over.' I choose my words carefully in case we're overheard. 'Wouldn't it be great if …' I pause, hoping she can hear it. 'If they could maybe get him into Europe, and he might have a home somewhere, like somewhere hot.

You know, I can imagine a villa with a veranda and … then we could visit him.' I don't want to admit how much I've fantasised about it.

She shakes her head. 'Dom, you're dreaming.'

'No, actually, I think it's possible. I mean they've got money, haven't they? Somehow. And if you think about the best thing for Dad, and what he'd want and enjoy, that's it. A home somewhere with a garden, 'cause he loved the garden, in some place far away from any police or authorities. Probably rural.'

She hesitates. 'Dom, what are you doing?' she says quietly. 'Don't hope for anything, you know who he's with. It's not going to happen like that.'

I turn my eyes away from her and look down. I notice the lines between the paving stones and the tarmac on the road.

It's Thursday evening and I'm already longing for the weekend. It's been a bad day. Four customers complained about their coffees, Magda's in a foul mood, and Ollie keeps disappearing into the toilet. He's either texting, crying or throwing up. I sense his new relationship isn't going well, but I don't ask. Instead, I focus on clearing and wiping down tables. Outside, the rain hasn't stopped all day. And I miss Mary. I'll be seeing her in a couple of weeks, but right now that's too far away. A few customers are glued to their laptops and I tidy up around them. I glance at the moving images on one of their screens.

My breath stops. No, I tell myself, this can't be true. I look around; the world's gone hazy. I stare at the screen again. I can't see these things or read them like this, not as words and pictures on screens … it's just wrong. I turn to Magda but she isn't paying attention. I bolt outside. I don't even bother to tell her I'll be back in a moment. I race to the guy on the corner with his pile of free evening papers.

I grab one. The headline is brutal: 'Disciples Raided – Two Dead'. I scan the text; names jump out at me. Not Gil's, and not Gemma's. But Riley's been shot four times – he put up a fight but he's gone. And Dad … Brian Minster, the traitor, is dead. He was shot while running away, because that's what traitors do.

I drop the paper. My head spins, my vision blurs but I can't faint, not in the street. I lean on a wall, its cold brick against my body. My hand claws at it. I can hear a scream at the back of my head trying to find a way out. I start running.

'Fuck! No. No!' I shout. I won't accept it. They're wrong. It's a fabrication. A set-up. My father can't be dead.

I keep running. I stop at a shop to buy a SIM. My hands shake as I hand over the money, the change spilling onto the counter. Then I race home and up the stairs, grab my notebook and find their number.

I'm running again, down streets. I duck into an alleyway. I dial the number and scream. 'Tell me it's not true! Tell me it didn't happen! You can't have let it happen! My father! My father! You fucking bastard, you were meant to keep him safe.'

I listen, waiting on the reply. But there is only an automated voice. 'I'm sorry but the number you have dialled has not been recognised. I'm sorry but the number you have dialled has not been recognised.'

I crumple to my knees. I look up. Darkness and the endless tumult of rain.

Flint finds me in the alleyway. I don't know how. I shake my head, distraught. He's crying too or the rain has soaked his face. He doesn't say anything but hugs me.

'I don't know how I live now, Flint.'

He holds me tight against him.

'Why did I hope for something better?' I sob.

Somehow he gets me home and I collapse onto my bed. When I wake, Charley is hugging me, crying. I think of Hansel and Gretel. Brother and sister trapped by the witch. The world is eating us up.

'I don't know how I live now,' I mutter.

'It's over.' She weeps. 'Everything.'

The next day when I open my eyes they're sticky with congealed tears. My body is cramped; Charley is still lying beside me. She's awake, but I'm not sure if she's slept.

'I feel bleak,' she whispers. 'I didn't get to see him. I never got to say goodbye.'

I don't have the energy to speak out loud so I whisper into her head. '*I don't know why they set him free, not to let him die like that.*'

'No.'

'*Nothing … nothing's been achieved. Dad's whole life … just wasted and gone now forever.*'

We are quiet. We sleep a while then wake, speak a little and sleep again. Later, in the afternoon, I phone Magda. I tell her I've been sick, really ill and I'm sorry I left like I did yesterday.

'Did something happen?' she asks.

I can't tell her, but promise I'll be in Monday. I hear Charley talking to Jackson. Despite everything, we have to go on.

Aunt Rena contacts the authorities to demand her brother's body back. She's called in and questioned. She tells them she never cared for her brother, but common decency means she wants to take charge of his remains. And as for us, she's had no contact with us for years.

'Mum can still surprise me,' Flint says proudly. 'She talked bullshit for three and a half hours. She said she was trying to bore them to death.' He chuckles. 'She's the best.'

They release his body to her, and she suggests he's cremated and we scatter his ashes somewhere peaceful. 'Lord knows, he had little enough peace in his life.'

But I know he did have peace for the sixteen years we lived together. If it wasn't for LifeStar Corporation, if it wasn't for the government, he'd still be here now. If he'd taken another job, if he'd earned less money, if he'd had less of a conscience, he might still be here now. Instead, he went to the Disciples. My father achieved nothing going to them except his own death.

We agree to the cremation and Rena arranges it. She gets the ashes back in an urn. She reckons, if we wait a few months, it will be safe for us to come together and scatter them. She also starts the legal process to get possession of what Dad owned. She intends to sell his house and give us the money from it.

'They're not making it easy for me,' she tells us. 'It'll probably take years.'

I remember our old home, walk through its large airy rooms in my mind, and then stop myself remembering.

Mary sends me a package. I posted her the briefest note to tell her what happened. (I never use email for such things, you don't know who's looking in.) Of course, she saw the news, but I needed to tell her too. I couldn't write about what I was feeling, except to say there were too many emotions to describe.

I take her package up to my room and open it in private. I lay the contents carefully across my bed. There are several flowers pressed between two pieces of card. There are some stones from the loch we love, and a single feather that matches the one she gave me when she left London. I touch each item, feeling the fragility of the flowers, the smooth cool surface of the stones, while the feather produces a tingling sensation in my fingertips. There is a note: 'I love you. I know you are strong. Eagle Heart.'

I sit there a long time gazing at her gifts. 'I have listened to everything you've said.' I hear my father's voice in my memory. 'And the thing that comforts me most is knowing that in your life there are people who love you. Despite everything I've done, you have people in your life who love you.'

Then I listen to the silence in my room.

'We need to think about what we do now,' Charley whispers.

We're all in the kitchen, the others are out.

'Dad's dead and … I want things to be different. I don't want us to keep feeling that everything we do is related to what he did. We want our own future.'

Flint nods. 'Of course.'

'I want us to have a home, and not share it with people we don't even like. Somewhere where we can wake up in the morning and feel happier and safer, where it's private. We've been saving up …' She pauses, mulling something over, then continues. 'Jackson's suggested I model in some shots. The pay's really good and it could help us.'

'Jackson suggested that?' Flint asks.

She nods. 'It's for a food ad, some new milk alternative. I didn't mention it before, because talking about money and how good it would feel to be in an ad … somehow it felt wrong given everything that's happened. But now it could help us get out of this place.'

I'm quiet. I can barely think beyond tomorrow's cappuccinos let alone consider moving. But Flint's amenable.

'We could probably do it, but rents are so high. We'd have nothing spare. Not for an emergency.'

'There won't be any emergencies,' Charley says forcefully. 'We've lived through that. Now we get our lives back. I want to have a home.'

Flint turns to me.

'It would be good to get out of here,' I say. I've not been hiding my emotions well, which I know can't continue. Still, what Charley wants doesn't feel real.

'So we're agreed,' she says.

'We're agreed.' Flint smiles.

I nod in approval, hoping my feelings will catch up with them.

CHAPTER 11

Mary meets me at the station. Seeing her again, the world brightens. We don't say much as she drives but our fingers entwine. We enter their shop and Gregory nods on seeing me. I feel comforted; it's our new routine. Mary takes me upstairs to put my rucksack in her room. We stand there, quiet, for a few long moments. Her eyes search mine.

'You're sad, Dom.' Her expression is open and kind.

'No, I'm very glad to be here.'

'I know that,' she says with assurance, 'but, I mean I feel it … about your dad.'

I don't answer immediately. 'I can't fully explain how I feel … just it's like being empty. And everything he hoped for is gone.'

She takes my hands in hers. 'I still think of Mum every day,' she says quietly. 'Sometimes, I even think I see her. Just walking down the road ahead of me.'

We draw closer and hug, her body comforting against mine; she squeezes me to her.

'Dominic!' Gregory calls up. He must be at the bottom of the stairs. 'I could do with some help down here.'

I release my embrace. 'Your father's calling me,' I tell her.

'Oh, yes.' Her eyes glisten with amusement. 'He's got this particularly heavy box he'd like you to help him move. Apparently, it needs a man.'

'Lucky he's got me, then.'

We both laugh and go back down. Gregory has plenty for me to do, and the best thing is I don't even mind.

Later, Mary has a bath. It's dark outside and quiet. I sit in her bedroom surrounded by all the things that are just Mary. On the chair by her bed are some old floppy toys; they must be from when she was very young. One, in particular, a rabbit, has been loved to the point of being threadbare. On her desk are photos of us together. We're grinning or pulling faces at the camera. They make me smile. Then there's a picture of her sitting between Gregory and her mother. I look at it more closely. Her mother died young. She had cancer and was involved in a drug trial, one of LifeStar Corporation's. Gregory blamed them for her death and that's why he sympathises with the Disciples. I remember when we lived in his cottage and he told us about it. I had no idea then that one day we might have so much in common.

I look away from the photo and focus on Mary's laptop, her pens and pencils. There are schoolbooks on her shelves and then something else catches my attention. On the top shelf, higher than I can reach, is a half-hidden object. I stand on her desk chair to have a look.

'Shit.' That's not what I expected. I'm staring at a dead bird's wing: huge and perfectly preserved, its feathers shades of brown and cream. I shiver, intrigued and repulsed.

'Don't touch it.' Mary's voice is clear behind me. She's standing in the doorway, a bathrobe wrapped around her.

'No,' I say. 'I'm not. What is it?'

She comes into the room and I get down from the chair.

'It's a golden eagle's wing,' she says. 'I took the feathers I gave you from it.'

I'm surprised I never noticed it before. 'How did you get it?'

She sits on the bed. 'I found it after Mum died. I was walking in the hills and then there it was. Gruesome, really. Obviously, something awful had happened. Nothing kills a top predator like an eagle, except that is for human beings.' She pauses. 'I'm not sure what made me pick it up.'

I sit on the bed next to her.

'Dad went crazy when he saw it. He said there were sick people out there and they were breaking the law. He got his shotgun and he went out onto those hills.' She stops, remembering. 'He was full of rage, he missed Mum so much.'

I feel a sudden sympathy for Gregory.

'But he didn't shoot anybody?' I ask, although I already know the answer.

'No. Whoever had killed it was long gone. He just came back, and we cleaned up the wing and preserved it.'

'It's fragile,' I suggest, 'the eagle wing, that's why I can't touch it?'

'No,' she says, holding my gaze, 'because it's powerful.'

'Powerful?'

'Yes. I rarely touch it myself. Hardly ever, except when I took out the feather I took to London, and the one I sent you recently.'

I look at her. She's got a toy rabbit on her chair and a dead eagle's wing on her shelf. How do I make sense of that?

'Mary,' I whisper, 'you are very strange and beautiful. And sometimes … I have no idea how we're together.'

She smiles. 'Because you're also very strange and beautiful, Dom. You just don't realise it.'

I laugh. She grins, opens her bathrobe and lets it slide off her shoulders. She pushes me down on her bed and straddles my body.

I look at the stars through the window, still and bright in the otherwise black sky. Mary's body is snuggled into mine. I feel peaceful, calm. It's never dark enough in London to really see the stars like this. And then I remember the night of my seventeenth birthday when I watched the stars with

Gil. He drove me on his motorbike, like a maniac, up to the top of a hill. We were alone and, like now, I felt a great peace, there was no fear. It was a positive connection between us. I briefly wonder if he too is watching these same sparks of light. Probably not. And then it doesn't matter anyway; he's irrelevant now.

Mary stirs. She turns to me and follows my gaze. She smiles. 'You're happy.'

'Yes. I … I love it here with you.'

Charley, Flint and I meet Rena at the suggested place. It's a journey out of London. We are a small gathering of four. The stream is crystal clear as it runs beneath the wooden bridge we're standing on. The trees around us provide privacy. There isn't another person about.

My mouth feels dry. 'I know this sounds stupid,' I say, 'but do we tip them all in in one go, or bit by bit?'

'We do it handful by handful,' Rena says gently.

'I don't know if I can touch his remains like that.'

'It may help, Dom, if you do. It makes it more real. It's part of saying goodbye.'

Rena goes first. Her hand, so like Dad's, dips into the urn. She sprinkles the ashes on the running water below. We watch them disappear in the rapid flow. Charley hesitates so Flint goes next. Both he and Rena seem calm, concentrating. Perhaps they're saying some private prayer? Charley starts sobbing. She puts her hand in the urn and throws a handful of Dad's ashes onto the water. Then it's my turn. But suddenly, I can't say goodbye. Not like this, not at all. Too much is left undone.

'I can't do it,' I mutter.

Rena puts her arm around me. Flint is hugging Charley. Rena strokes my back gently, she's mumbling something comforting although I've no idea what it is. She gradually takes my hand and guides it to the urn. I feel the fineness of the ash as my fingers touch it. She helps me take a scoop and then together we throw it into the water. We repeat another round of the ritual and then do it again. Charley grows calmer. I pick up the ashes on my own. Eventually, they're all gone.

The water continues flowing. A light breeze rustles the leaves of the trees. We are in a place full of green and bark, of water and stone; it's peaceful. And finally I realise I can still feel close to Dad. His ashes are gone, but what remains is what of him is inside me. Charley and me. He'd loved us, and that still exists.

The estate agent opens the door and we all walk in. It's the fourth potential flat to rent we've looked at today. I'm tired. I've had enough. They're all further away from central London than our current house share, which means a longer journey to work, and each one has been a heart sink. I wish we had more money. Charley's plan is falling apart.

'I think you'll particularly like this,' the guy says, walking us into the large open-plan living room, kitchen and diner. We've already seen the long narrow hallway, the one double bedroom off it, and the small single room that just takes a bed and chest of drawers. The bathroom's in the middle. The flat is clean and the windows in this open-plan area make it feel bright and spacious. We all perk up. It's definitely the best we've seen.

'And as I said,' the estate agent continues, 'for the space it's very well priced. The owner did it up. He was hoping to sell it, but now he just wants it occupied. It'll go quickly so if you like it, I'd make your decision as fast as you can. He's prepared to leave it furnished.' He withdraws into the hallway while we consider it.

'It's good,' Charley says quietly. 'I love this part.' She

walks over to look out of the windows. 'There's even trees outside.'

I can tell Flint likes it too. He turns to me. 'Do you think you can live with that bedroom?'

I realise I've drawn the short straw. Charley waits on my reply.

'I'd have trouble swinging a cat in it.'

'Yeah,' he agrees. 'It's small.'

'But … overall, this is the best place we've seen.'

'Definitely,' Charley says with conviction. 'And you could take some space in our wardrobe.'

I consider the single bed, but it doesn't really matter because I'll be seeing Mary at her place.

'Let's go for it,' I say.

Charley hugs me and plants a kiss on my cheek. 'Thank you, Dom.'

We go back to the house share, call the landlord and hand in our notice. My sister is happy. 'We can make it a real home.'

Two days before we move a letter arrives addressed to me. I don't recognise the handwriting and the envelope is sealed so tightly I have to use a knife to open it. I shut the door of my room to read it. There is a single sheet of paper enclosed.

I am truly sorry for your loss.
Keep your head down and out of sight.
I promise you we shall avenge his death.
Take care, my friend.
If you need me … then an eleven-digit mobile number.

Panic. I fold it over quickly; it isn't even typed. What is Gil doing? But then a handwritten letter looks personal, there's less chance of someone else opening it in error. The panic subsides and then I feel sad. Is he trying to offer me sympathy? Advice? He should have kept my father alive – I don't need his sympathy. He should be looking for the person who betrayed him, not writing me letters. He knew how much I loved my father. I almost tear the note into pieces. I should flush it down the toilet. And I can't tell Charley or Flint about it. I look at the packed boxes containing all I own. We're moving. We're going to something better. Why? Why did he have to call me 'my friend'?

Much later, I write the number in my notebook. It means nothing without a name attached to it. Eleven digits floating on a page. I take the letter into the kitchen. Everyone has gone to bed. I put on one of the gas rings, light the paper and, holding it over the sink, I watch it burn and disintegrate.

CHAPTER 12

On Saturday, we move into the new flat. We spend the day transporting and unpacking our stuff, and that night I fall asleep quickly in my new room. The next day, I'm up first. I walk into the kitchen and the surfaces seem to shine they're so clean. I catch myself listening out for Spider and the others, and then remember I don't need to. We've no unwanted housemates now. No one to overhear our private conversations. I can just be Dom; Luke belongs at work. Even my tiny room is the best place I've had for years.

I stand in the hallway feeling happier than I thought I would. Charley and Flint's door is ajar and I can hear Flint snoring. It's the loudest I've heard him. I tiptoe to their room, carefully push the door open and sneak inside. Standing by Flint's side of the bed, I lean over and gently tickle the end of his nose with my finger. He snuffles and twitches. I hold back until he's still. I tickle him again and then, without knowing when he woke, he's suddenly got me in a headlock. I'm half laughing, half struggling to breathe and somehow Charley continues sleeping. Flint's out of bed and dragging me into the living room. He throws me on the sofa. All I can do is laugh.

'You could wake half of London,' I protest.

He grabs a cushion and hits me with it. 'I was sleeping – you woke me up.'

'I'm sorry,' I say, but couldn't sound less apologetic.

He whacks me again, the cushion almost bursts, then he sits on the sofa beside me.

'Shit, Dom.' He sighs. 'Is this what you're gonna be like now? 'Cause if you are, I'm gonna write to Mary. She needs to be here weekends to keep you entertained. If you're gettin' laid, I'll get to sleep.'

'Is it that simple?' I ask. 'I'm sure I'd find another way to wind you up.'

'Probably,' he says, 'but at least it'd be later in the day.'

I watch his face. He seems very serious.

'You're not mad at me are you?' I ask.

'I should be,' he says then shakes his head slowly. 'Nah.'

He leans over to ruffle my hair like I'm some big kid. I missed us fooling around like this in the house share.

Flint glances across at the doorway; Charley's still not up. He goes and gets tobacco and Rizla paper out of his jacket pocket and starts to roll a cigarette. The general rule is he doesn't smoke indoors, but it's Charley who insists on it. I watch him ease the tobacco along the paper, then he crosses the room again to get a little extra, just to keep us real chilled. He rolls it up and licks down the edge.

I open the window near us. He lights up and shares it with me. I don't take that many drags on it, and we both exhale out the window. When we're finished, we let fresh air in to banish any lingering smell, and we've closed the window before Charley stands in the doorway bleary eyed.

'What time did you get up?' she asks.

'When your brother decided he was bored,' Flint says with a grin.

Charley throws the magazine onto the table, flicks through the pages and leaves it open for us. 'Take a look.'

Flint and I gaze down at the photo advertisement. It's Charley but not as we've ever seen her before. She's wearing a brightly coloured polka-dot dress and her make-up is exaggerated; it's a half real, half cartoon image.

'I thought they were gonna make you look beautiful?' Flint says.

'So did I. Not like some girly airhead.'

I chuckle. 'You mean not like you're "Nutz for All-Nutz"?'

'My one time in an ad and I look like this.' She shakes her head.

'That's cool,' Flint says, 'I don't need too many guys eyeing you.'

'And they've paid you a fortune,' I remind her. 'People are asking for it at work so it's doing a good job.'

'I just ...' She looks at the photo and sighs. 'I don't know. I just thought maybe it could be the start of something ... you know like I might be a model. But obviously this is what advertisers think I'm good for.'

'Charley, most models are too skinny, they have eating disorders. I don't want to see you like that,' I say.

Flint nods.

'And really, at base,' I say, 'it's about female exploitation and objectification.' As soon as I've said it I know I've gone too far.

She snaps back sharply. 'Don't quote Gil Zimmerman to me, Dom. Talk about exploitation – he was the master of it.'

I look down. My cheeks are hot. How could I have said that?

'I'm not a stupid woman and I can make my own choices.'

'Of course, Charley.'

I feel her eyes on me, furious.

'I'm sorry, okay? I'm sorry.'

She shakes her head again then says more gently, 'Don't you understand, Dom? What upsets me most is that he's still in your head. All those hours we had to listen to them lecturing us and it's still in your head.'

I know nothing I say is going to make this better.

'Hey,' Flint says. 'We don't need to go over this. Let's just celebrate you're in that ad. It's done us good. We don't need to analyse it.'

'Yeah,' I agree. 'I'm proud of you, Charley.' I make an effort to smile and she relents. She even lets me hug her.

Over the next few weeks, Charley starts bringing home brochures about evening classes from the local colleges.

'I think I could get my A levels like this,' she says. 'If I take all the sciences that should get me into medical school.'

'Charley, you'll get them with ease,' I say. I'm impressed at how she's focusing on the future.

'Will you start practising the sax again?' she asks.

I shrug.

'You should start playing again,' she says. 'You were good, Dom. You could be even better now, if you put in the effort.

'Okay,' I say softly. 'I'll think about putting in the effort.'

'Yeah, Dom,' Flint says. 'I never hear you play these days and I remember you were good.'

'Will you play for *us*, Dom?' Charley asks. I know she's pushing me but I also know she's right to.

'I'll play for you.'

I start practising again. Maybe, finally, we both have a future that's our own.

Monday morning. The queue at Coffee Primo is going out the door.

'I told Magda this would happen,' Ollie says. 'Café Terrazza's closed, some big refit 'cause it's expanding. I said they'd come here instead.'

'I don't get it,' I say, 'they've got other places closer to them.'

'Yeah, but our coffee's better,' Ollie says like he wishes it wasn't; he can't be bothered.

I look at the long line of customers. They want their caffeine fix and they want it quick, but there's only the three of us.

'Oh shit,' I say under my breath, aware some in the queue are wearing LifeStar Corporation ID cards. I'll just keep my head down and focus on the coffee.

It is manic. Ollie takes the orders while Magda and I race to produce enough cappuccinos and lattes. I scald my hand in the rush and yelp.

'Flush it with cold water,' says a tall, slim man. He has dark hair flecked with grey. I've seen similar clean-shaven faces and well-cut suits before, but they never notice me.

'I'm okay,' I lie, because I can't leave the counter.

He waits a moment as our eyes meet. His are grey-green in colour. 'I'd like a medium cappuccino,' he says, looking at my hand wrapped in kitchen towel. 'Just one shot, and take your time. It's not worth an injury.'

When I pass him his coffee, I notice he's carrying a large leather holdall and his wedding ring glistens.

'Hey, I take the orders,' Ollie hisses. 'You make the coffees.'

The guy gives me a brief nod, turns and walks away.

On Thursday evening, I'm clearing up at the end of the day, collecting cups and wiping down tables when I notice the man again. He's leaning back on the comfy sofa, his eyes closed. I register the leather bag by his feet, his manicured hands, neatly combed hair and expensive suit. He must work in finance, there's something obvious about his wealth. I go to quietly pick up the discarded cup and plate of crumbs near him. I load the tray and then notice his eyes are open, watching me.

'How's your hand?' he asks.

I feel my cheeks redden. 'It's okay … it was just a minor scald.'

He sits up straighter and looks at me quizzically. 'You

worked in Café Terrazza, right? I'm sure I've seen you before.'

'No.' I shake my head. 'I've never worked in Café Terrazza.'

'How long you been here then?'

'Er … about six months,' I say.

'Okay.' He nods yet his eyes stay on me. I pick up the tray and bring the conversation to a close.

Every couple of days he comes in. I don't quite know how it happens but one way or another we have some kind of interaction. Even if I'm not making his coffee, he comes back to the counter and wants something from me.

'Would you mind adding a bit more hot milk to this,' or 'I'm sure I asked for one shot and this tastes like two.'

His style is too friendly for me to say he's an unhappy customer, but he's demanding. I imagine he runs a department somewhere in a big office and the staff who work for him are constantly on their toes.

'Thanks,' he'll say. 'You've been very helpful.'

He's always polite and even makes an effort to chat a bit; most people don't bother with that.

'I'll have a one-shot decaf tonight. I'm off to the gym so nothing too strong.'

'One-shot decaf coming up,' I say.

'You go to the gym?' he asks.

I shake my head and let the steam heat the milk. 'No, I don't like working out.'

'Well, you're lucky you're young enough not to have to go to the gym if you don't want to.' He smiles. 'That's the joy of being – what are you, eighteen? Nineteen?'

'Eighteen,' I say.

'Ah, a great age. At eighteen, I didn't care for working out either. Too busy getting into girls and music.'

'Oh, yeah, what music were you into?' I can't help asking.

'Okay, I'll tell you but don't laugh. It's not trendy. Jazz.'

I smile. 'Jazz is cool. Sometimes it's trendy.'

'You're the only young person I've heard say that.'

'Then maybe you don't know enough young people.' I hand him his coffee.

He walks to a table near the window and Ollie sidles over.

'That guy fancies you,' he says in a low voice.

'What?' I turn to him.

'He can't keep his eyes off you.'

'Nobody fancies me, Ollie,' I say quickly.

'Really?' He chuckles. 'He just happens to make a beeline for you every time he's in here. And even now,' he gestures, 'his eyes are coming right this way.' He grins.

'Nobody fancies me,' I say firmly.

He raises his eyebrows, sceptical. 'Like you'd know. You're cute, Luke, but very naïve.'

I walk away. I'm not listening to any more but my cheeks are hot. I check out the sandwiches in the refrigerated unit, glad for the cool. When I get back behind the counter I dare to glance across at the window. He's looking down at his phone then rummaging through his holdall. Am I naïve? Don't I understand what's happening around me? I swallow hard feeling flustered again.

He takes out an old pair of trainers and an A4 lever arch file. He's obviously looking for something, then he's putting his things back. He gets up to go but there's something he's missed on the floor. Despite Ollie, I feel obliged to tell him. 'You've dropped something,' I say as he passes by, and I motion to where he was sitting.

He looks back and goes to retrieve it.

'Thanks,' he says, 'I can't lose this.'

I see it briefly before he puts it in his pocket. An ID card with a photo and his title. I can't read it properly but I can make out one thing clearly – the company he works for: LifeStar Corporation. A chill runs down my spine as I watch him walk away.

CHAPTER 13

He doesn't come into Coffee Primo again. Café Terrazza reopens and takes its customers back. I won't admit to anyone just how relieved I am. I don't have to listen to any more jibes from Ollie, and more importantly I don't have to face talking to someone from LifeStar Corporation. I think I spy him one lunchtime looking through the window with a woman by his side. Her hat is drawn low across her face, but the rain is pelting down so maybe it's not him at all; it's hard to tell in the rain.

Friday evening I leave work as usual, glad for the weekend ahead. One advantage of working in this branch is we're closed weekends. Magda locks up and I take the rubbish bags round the back to the commercial bins. The alley stinks of rotting food and piss. As I close the lid, I hear a voice behind me.

'Dominic Minster.'

I freeze.

'I know who you are.' I recognise his voice.

I'm trapped; if he's standing behind me I can't get past him. I turn to him slowly. 'I'm sorry,' I say, holding my voice as steady as I can, 'but I'm Luke Giddens.'

'You're also Dominic Minster.' He's standing opposite but I won't meet his eyes. 'I worked with your father,' he says slowly, 'and you're very like him in a lot of ways.'

My thoughts spin. Now I understand why he was talking to me; he's been figuring out who I am.

'I suspected it for a while,' he says, 'and Janice, who you'll remember, confirmed it for me. Considering the amount of time she used to spend in your home, she does remember you well.'

I'm speechless. Janice was my father's girlfriend for years, a colleague from LifeStar, but she betrayed him in the press.

'She loved your father,' he says, 'and she told me she liked you a lot too.'

'She betrayed my father,' I retort. 'She told the media a lot of lies. Bullshit. You don't do that to people you love.'

'No,' he agrees. 'You don't … unless you're put under an inordinate amount of pressure to denounce them.'

I shake my head. 'I shouldn't be talking to you.'

'Why? What am I going to do to you, Dominic? I'm only a colleague of your father's.'

I raise my eyes to meet his.

'A colleague? Perhaps. But … you might also be working for the police or MI5.'

He laughs. 'Good God, you've got some imagination. They don't employ people like me.'

'They might.'

His laughter stops. 'You really are afraid, aren't you?'

'Didn't you read the news? My father's dead. He worked for LifeStar Corporation. Why shouldn't I be afraid? I've no idea who you are but you know who I am.'

He looks at me, bemused. 'It wasn't LifeStar Corporation who killed your father, but his involvement with the Disciples. And I'm Dr Ian Pendleton.'

I stand there hostile and afraid. He withdraws his security ID and passes it to me. It's an enhanced ID card with his photo and title: Dr Ian Pendleton, Research Manager and Advisor – Genetics.'

I feel sick. My father was a research manager and advisor. I pass it back but my hand shakes slightly. He's quite relaxed. 'What is it you want?' I ask.

'To talk to you, if you'll let me. I wouldn't mind buying you a drink.'

'Why would you want to do that?'

'I worked closely with your father and … when he was arrested, I found it most disconcerting. Indeed, I've never fully understood what happened. And I find I'd like to talk about it.'

Looking at him, I think it's possible he's telling the truth, but I can't know.

'I'm sorry,' I say. 'But you'll have to excuse me. The police were once looking for me, my picture was in the papers. You may prefer to hand me in. I can't trust you.'

'If I wanted to hand you in, I'd have done it by now. Isn't that rather obvious?' he says matter-of-factly. 'And as it happens, I think the police were wrong, very wrong, to ever bring you or your sister into it – you had nothing to do with it.' He pauses and I sense him gauging what to say next. 'I imagine you miss your father,' he says softly. 'And I suspect,' his eyes focus on my name badge, 'Luke doesn't talk about him, but maybe Dominic would like to. Of course, if it makes you feel more comfortable, I can call you Luke.'

There is truth in what he's saying – if he'd wanted to hand me in he could have. He stands still waiting on my response, and there's nothing threatening about him. For the briefest moment, Gil flashes through my mind. And then my fear alters. I'm intrigued. What will he say? More importantly, what might I learn?'

'You can call me Luke,' I say.

'And you can call me Ian.'

We walk to a local boozer. It's crowded with people, hardly the place for an intimate chat. I feel safe enough.

'This pub,' Ian says, 'goes back to the days of King Charles the Second.'

'They must sell good beer then.' It's as close to a joke as I can manage. He smiles and buys me a pint. We squeeze into a corner; there's nowhere else to sit.

'Your father,' he starts, 'was one of the most brilliant men I've ever known. You probably didn't realise it, but his mind was … his thoughts were ahead of everyone else.' He talks loudly, it's the only way to be heard.

'I don't know about that,' I say. 'He never talked about work. We kind of knew it was a subject off-limits. You guys all sign a secrecy act. But …' I shrug. 'I'll take your word for it.'

'To be honest, I've found it difficult to accept what happened to him. I even wondered once if he was being stitched up. It was a way of removing him from his job. LifeStar's a competitive place and …' He takes a sip of his drink. 'I couldn't believe he'd had anything to do with the Disciples. But after that raid on Colchester House, I realised he must have.'

How can he just say that out loud? I gaze around quickly but everybody else seems engrossed in their own conversation; it's hard to hear them anyway. I watch him take another gulp of his beer. He seems so ordinary, dressed in his suit. His hair is a little dishevelled like he's tired or been racking his brains over his desk.

'If only Brian had known what we learnt afterwards,' he says quietly.

I listen carefully. I realise he wants to talk, for whatever reason. I don't have to say much back. I take a few sips of my own drink.

'LifeStar monitors any information you take off their computer system. Any memory stick that goes into your laptop, any research papers you take home to read, it's all monitored and logged. We had no idea – but after your father was arrested, they let us know.'

My stomach contracts. 'That's not normal practice in a company is it?'

'No.' He shakes his head. 'It's not. But they told us to warn off anyone thinking of something similar. Don't get

me wrong, I think they're right to do that, of course, but …
if only Brian had known, maybe he'd still be with us. Things
would be different.'

I imagine my father saving document after confidential
document onto a memory stick, and doing everything he
could to hide it. Yet it was there, right in front of LifeStar,
every bit of information he took. Information the Disciples
never received. I'm too shocked to say any more; I feel I've
been punched in the stomach.

After a while, Dr Pendleton says, 'I guess it must have
been pretty hard for you too?'

I nod. I have an overwhelming desire to go. I should
walk out of there, I don't want to hear this. Yet my legs feel
frozen. I have to appear normal.

'Yes,' I say, 'he was there every day in our lives and then
he was gone. We got back from school, and the house was
just a wreck.'

He looks at me. 'I don't suppose anything can prepare
you for something like that.'

'No.' I have to watch every word I say. 'That's why we
ran. We knew something really bad had happened and
instinct took over.'

'It must have been terrifying,' he says sympathetically.

'And then everything we read afterwards, it was like a
nightmare. You know, the idea that he was involved with the
Disciples. We read stuff and it couldn't be real because none
of it related to Dad, not *our* dad.'

'Yes, that's how we felt at the time, his colleagues. And
Janice was really cut up.'

I take a few gulps of beer. But swallowing, my throat is
tight. 'Listen,' I say, 'thanks for the drink but I really need to
go.' I put down my pint and leave quickly.

I stop in a side road near the station. Giddy, I lean against
a wall. I might be sick. I remember Janice, the picture Dad
had in his study of the two of them together. All the times

she stayed over. I thought she betrayed him but maybe she mourned him too? We got on well when she spent weekends with us. I never loved her, but I can see her differently now.

And what I've just learnt about LifeStar Corporation, it's a terrible truth. They're like a security service in themselves, monitoring everything taken off and saved from its computer system. Was my father doomed before he even made contact with the Disciples? Was Gil Zimmerman irrelevant from the start? It's unbearable.

'Dominic, I'm sorry. I upset you.'

I jump. It's Dr Pendleton. Why's he followed me?

'I wasn't very sensitive, was I?' he says, apologetic.

'I need to go home.' I push by him to walk away.

'Wait. I have your father's things, what was left in his office. I thought you might want them.'

I turn to him, my anger shrinking. 'What?'

'They're not on me, obviously. But I've kept them. I always hoped there would be someone to give them to.'

He looks tired and serious; he's older than I realised. Is that a good thing? Maybe he's the same age as my father?

'There's not much: a book, some photos, a pen. They took most of what he had away, but these were his private things.'

I stand there trying to take it in. 'I … I would like them. Yes.'

'Are you free Sunday afternoon?' he asks. 'If you're free you could pop round and I can give you them.'

'You mean come to your home?'

'Well, that's where I've got them.'

I don't respond immediately. But then he gives me his address and suggests a time. Eventually, I agree to it then quickly go home.

CHAPTER 14

I pace the room describing what happened. Charley and Flint sit on the sofa, listening.

'I feel better about it now,' I say, sitting down opposite them. 'I think Dr Pendleton's okay. I ... definitely think he's okay.'

'You don't know that,' Flint says slowly.

'And he's doing Dad's job,' Charley says, 'working on the same projects he was. I don't like it at all.'

Flint watches me. 'I also don't get it. Why can't he just bring your dad's stuff into Coffee Primo? Why does he want you to go round?'

'Well ...' I say, thinking, 'I guess it's more personal, and I wouldn't want him to bring them into work. Magda and Ollie would ask too many questions.' I don't want to go into how Ollie's been recently.

Flint isn't convinced. 'Your dad's dead. He was branded a traitor. And this guy's asking you round. Shit, Dom. He's LifeStar management, his place'll cost millions. Why's he doin' it? To give you a book and a few photos?'

'Flint, I think what happened to Dad, it got to him. And now, maybe he just wants to show some kindness to a colleague's son. Can't that be the case? And anyway, we used to live in an expensive home too.' We're quiet. 'I want those things back,' I whisper, 'and I've agreed to meet him now.'

'You don't have to go,' Charley says quietly.

'I think I do. It won't look good if I don't turn up. At best he'll think I'm rude. At worst he could start considering things he hasn't even thought of yet.'

Charley's eyes are full of concern. 'Dom, how has this happened? We've spent all this time using pseudonyms, hiding our identities, and now Dr Pendleton, *Research Manager and Advisor*,' she stresses, 'knows who you are. You've been in some pub discussing Dad, and …' She shakes her head, upset.

'Charley, the guy started talking to me at work. He figured out who I was. He had me practically trapped in an alleyway. What was I supposed to do?'

'I don't know,' she says loudly. 'But … maybe you shouldn't have taken that job at Coffee Primo? I mean, if you think about it, it's too close to LifeStar.'

'What? Charley, no. It was the best job I'd been offered. Remember, we were all just happy I'd got it. And if Café Terrazza hadn't closed, he'd never have come in.'

'I'm scared. Okay?' She's really upset. 'I'm scared, Dom.'

There is a tense silence.

'Do you want to come too?' I ask her. 'Then you'll meet him and see for yourself. He's alright.'

'I was wondering that,' she says, thoughtful.

'No way,' Flint says firmly. 'He can't know any more about you, and nothing about Charley. We deal with this the best we can. Get your dad's stuff, Dom, tell him a load of bullshit, and get the hell out.'

'Okay,' I agree, my eyes on Charley.

She turns to Flint and nods.

I find Pendleton's place with ease, a large three-storey town house. When he opens the door I can see he's got a beautiful home. We walk through the hallway into his living room. There are large works of contemporary art on the walls

– paintings of swirls and blocks of colour – and unusual sculpted objects sit on shelves.

'Wow.' I can't hold back. 'You've an amazing place.'

'My wife's an art dealer. On occasion we buy some ourselves.'

'I've … never seen anything like it.' It's not art I'd normally like, but hanging on his walls it makes sense.

He smiles. 'She's got good taste.'

I wonder if that's why he's invited me here, to show off. 'It's like you're living in an art gallery.'

He laughs. 'Well, it's just home to me.'

It's obvious everything in his living room is expensive. There are two enormous leather sofas and a few individual armchairs, both of which look antique. It's a strange contrast between the old and the new, yet it works.

'Can I get you something to drink?' he asks politely.

'Yeah, a juice if you've got one.'

'Cranberry or orange?'

'Orange, thanks.'

He disappears into the kitchen which I briefly see is huge and open plan, very modern and stylish.

He returns and passes me a glass of orange juice with ice in it. He's got himself a mineral water. We each sit on a sofa, across from one another.

'So where do you live, Luke?'

I've prepared my answers; I'll lie well. 'Compared to this, where I live is a little shit hole on the other side of London. A bedsit. I don't like it but it's all I can afford.'

'And you live there alone?' He loves to ask questions.

'Yeah … I had a girlfriend, but it didn't work out. So now I live there alone.' I try to sound relaxed, but I'm on guard.

'And do you still have contact with your sister?'

I've rehearsed what to say about Charley most. 'We were close for a while, but I don't see her now. She … she got involved with some bloke, I didn't like him. I mean, I feel protective towards her, and he wasn't a good guy, but she couldn't see it, and there was no way we could all keep hanging out with each other.'

'Do you know where she is?'

'Somewhere in Leeds, I think.'

'So she won't get to see what I'm giving you?' he says softly.

'Probably not.'

He looks at me curiously. I hope he believes me. 'You must be quite lonely.'

Somehow, those words catch me off guard. 'I miss my father,' I say slowly.

'Yes. I'm sure you do.'

'And now, I'll never see him again.'

'No, death is always final. I lost my own father six years ago and … it's funny how, even as an adult, and after all this time, I still have moments when I miss him. When I think, "Oh, I wish he were here to see that".'

'Are you saying I'll never stop missing him?'

'A part of you probably won't.'

We are so different and yet maybe he does understand. 'That's what I think too,' I say.

'I confess, I never really thought of your father as someone who had many friends. Maybe many geniuses don't. And I do wonder if I should have made more of an effort to be one. Perhaps then … things could have worked out differently.' He shrugs. 'But of course, I don't know.'

I've never heard anyone speak about my father like that. 'He wasn't lonely,' I insist.

'Probably not. But he was a loner. Sometimes I'd say, quite a maverick one.'

I sense how many directions the conversation could go in, but none of them feel safe. I don't say anything else.

Eventually, he gets up and opens one of the doors in

the long sideboard against the wall. He withdraws a tattered-looking book, a couple of picture frames and a pen. He puts them on the coffee table before me. These are my father's things. I pick up the book first. A King James Bible, the last thing I'd expect to see. It's part of a Classics series, a regular paperback, not an old-fashioned leather-bound book. I carefully flick through it. The pages appear to have been well read, or used, but there are no markings anywhere except for one passage in orange highlighter.

And He shall judge among the nations, and shall rebuke many people: and they shall beat their swords into ploughshares, and their spears into pruning hooks: nation shall not lift up sword against nation, neither shall they learn war any more.

'I don't understand,' I mutter.
Pendleton is quiet, watching me.
'He wasn't a religious man,' I say.
'I never thought of him as that, no.'
'I don't understand,' I say, growing anxious, 'why this was left in his office. The police reported that he used biblical quotes to communicate with the Disciples, so why would they leave this Bible? It's evidence.'
Pendleton's face is impassive. 'It's a Bible, Dominic. One of the most easily accessed books in the world. You can download it free from the internet, you can look up any quote you want. Why would they take it?'
I stop myself asking any more, afraid I've already given too much away.
'He was an atheist,' I whisper, turning to the photos. My hands are shaking slightly. I close my eyes a moment and swallow hard; these are the images my father chose to have sitting in his office. All the pictures of our childhood were left behind in our home and lost forever on his confiscated computers.

I hear Pendleton rise and open my eyes quickly. 'I'll leave you alone a moment,' he says, and quietly leaves the room.

In the first photograph, Dad is standing between Charley and me. We're on a skiing holiday, smiling at the camera. We're in down jackets and goggles rest on our heads. Our faces are full of colour, the air obviously cold. It was a lifetime ago. The second shot is even older. Charley and I both sit on a beach towel in matching pale blue swimsuits. We look so young; how old were we then? Nine or ten. Yet Dad must have loved this photo to frame it and keep it in his office. And then there's his pen. A gold fountain pen. I can't remember ever seeing it; it must have been something he got for work, maybe to sign documents. It's such an old-fashioned thing I'm surprised he had it. I look at the four objects. What did I expect to get or feel?

Pendleton comes back into the room. I know I'm close to crying. I ask if I can go to the bathroom. He shows me to the downstairs toilet. It's spotlessly clean with an old vintage circus sign hanging on the wall. I pee, blow my nose and splash some water on my face. I take my time. When I come out I gather up Dad's few belongings, thank Pendleton and leave. I feel exhausted. I want to go home and sleep.

CHAPTER 15

Charley and I sit on the sofa. She looks at each of Dad's things.

'These don't make me feel any better,' she says quietly. 'It wasn't worth going.'

'Don't say that, Charley. We don't have any other photos from our childhood.'

She gazes at the one of us sitting on the beach and shakes her head sadly. 'You go back into work tomorrow, and you have nothing more to do with Dr Pendleton. These things are private – he should never have had them in the first place.'

It strikes me Pendleton could have binned them, and he was doing us a favour, but I don't say it. I walk over to the small bookshelf we have and place the items on top. Flint stares at the photos a while; he's not seen pictures of us so young.

'You looked so alike then,' he says. 'If you'd been the same sex … maybe you'd be identical twins.'

Neither of us comment. We're different now. We leave the items on the bookshelf and, as the days pass, it's amazing how quickly we barely even register them. They blend into the background, the episode with Pendleton over.

Three weeks later, I return from lunch and there's a note for me.

I'd like to speak to you – it's important. How about after work on Friday? Let me know. Ian.

Oh, no. He's given me his mobile number but there's no way I will ring it. I hope he'll get the message: we're not meeting again.

I leave work Friday evening. I'm thinking about the film Charley and I want to see this weekend and suddenly he's crossing the road. For a moment I consider running off, but that isn't an option. Instead, I address him directly. 'Dr Pendleton, I'm sorry but I've a busy weekend. I'm going home.'

'I won't keep you long,' he says, 'but I'd like to ask you a favour.' He looks very serious. 'Perhaps in return … I can do you one.'

'I really need to get home.'

'Please, just listen to me, and then you can think about it. I won't take long. If you can't meet now then what about Tuesday night?'

I have a horrible feeling he's not going to back off; I also know the power he potentially has over me. 'I'm meeting a friend shortly,' I lie, buying time. How do I handle him? Maybe it's safer to meet him than not. I don't want him coming into Coffee Primo again. 'I've … a little time Tuesday evening,' I say quietly.

He nods but doesn't look any happier.

I don't tell Charley or Flint about him. They'll blame me for his persistence. What I need to do is face him head-on and be completely blunt: I don't want him to contact me again, and in memory of my father I hope he'll respect that.

On Tuesday evening we go to a pub. It's a different one from last time and quiet. I let him buy me half a pint. We sit and he gets straight to the point.

'I have a stepson,' he says slowly. 'Justin. He's a bright and intelligent boy, second year university, not much older than you, but … he's a concern at the moment.'

I look at his smart suit and think of his beautiful home. Why is he telling me this? I glance at the clock on the wall. I'll give him ten minutes, no more.

'Our relationship hasn't always been easy,' he says. 'He was ten when I met his mother and I understand he saw me as a threat. I've had to work hard with him.'

'Dr Pendleton ...' I interrupt softly.

'Ian,' he insists.

'Ian, I'm sorry but I don't see what this has got to do with me.'

His voice drops to a whisper. 'I'm afraid he's going to join the Disciples.' His eyes are full of anxiety. 'He spends hours reading about them, consuming information, propaganda, and now he's saying things that I can only call disturbing. I can't ignore them.'

My heart starts racing. The seat beneath me seems to sway. 'Then you need to speak to the police,' I say, holding my voice as steady as I can.

'I'm sure you can understand I want to avoid that,' he says carefully. 'My wife and I have been doing what we can to contain the situation. We're not funding him to live away from home this year, it helps us keep an eye on him, but he needs an injection of reality. I think if he spoke to someone like you, someone of a similar age who has direct experience of the damage the Disciples cause, he might come to his senses. He'll see through the nonsense he's been reading online. And he'll understand that it's not a game.'

'I can't help you,' I say quickly. 'I can't talk about this. I hate the Disciples. They helped destroy my father.' I stand up to go. I have to get out of here. What kind of mistake did I make going to his house that day? Does he think now he can involve me in his personal matters?

'That's why I hoped you'd speak to him,' he says urgently. 'You know how much the Disciples hurt people. I really need your help. He's ...' I hear the desperation in his voice. 'If I can offer you something in return – money or a job contact, a university reference – I'd be glad to give it.'

'Ian, I'm sorry.' I'm trying to control my panic. 'He's your son. He's got nothing to do with me. You need to speak to him. Your colleague's dead, the facts say it all, you don't need me to explain them. Please don't approach me again.'

'But he won't listen to me.'

They're the last words I hear before I bolt from the pub. I run. He's not going to catch up this time. I've made myself clear. When I reach the station I dart inside and rush for the Tube. The doors close behind me. I watch the passengers on the platform. He's not there but I'm shaking. The bullet wound in my shoulder aches. I feel it screaming – Disciple.

A young man walks into Coffee Primo. I've never seen him before but some internal radar alerts me to danger. He looks like someone posing, imitating the style of the Disciples. Faded jeans, khaki T-shirt, and an old-looking army surplus jacket. He has hair he's starting to grow long and piercings in both his ears. His eyes fix on me. They lack the determination I've seen in the Disciples' eyes, but still, he makes me very uneasy. He lets other customers go before him ensuring he places his order with me. A two-shot cappuccino and roasted veg panini. I put it in the toaster, aware I have to take it to his table.

He sits near the window. His phone and student ID are on the table, face up. I read his name and baulk. Justin Pendleton. He doesn't speak until I put his sandwich down.

'My father says he'll give me two hundred and fifty pounds if I talk to you for thirty minutes.' He smiles but it isn't friendly. 'That's over eight pounds a minute. He said he'd pay you too.'

I'm shocked. He's like a spoilt child. I don't respond.

'I should think it's more than they pay you here,' he says. 'For a whole day if not the week.'

My mouth feels dry. 'I'm sorry,' I mutter, 'but your father

doesn't buy me, and neither can you.'

He watches me and then says slowly. 'Ian said the Disciples all but killed your father, but when I did my research on him, I'd say it was LifeStar Corporation that killed him.'

My breath stops in my throat. Who does he think he is to say that? He speaks with such ease, and without any care as to who might hear, yet I'm at work.

'You don't know anything,' I whisper, afraid.

'No?'

He's a customer, I have to watch what I do; I feel trapped. I drop my voice even lower. 'Leave me alone. I have nothing to say to you.' Then I turn and walk off. I feel his eyes on my back. I don't look at him again.

The next day, he returns. My heart sinks. He orders a coffee and panini from Ollie and sits near the window. His eyes keep flitting across to me. I try to ignore him but my skin prickles. What is it about the Pendletons that makes them think they can treat me like this? I'm fuming but I'm also scared. The following day, he's back again and orders from me. I have to face him when I take his sandwich to him. I keep my eyes down and place the panini on his table.

'Have I upset you?' he asks plainly. 'I'm sorry, I'm like that at times. I piss people off. I don't mean to, but …' He shrugs. 'Maybe I take after my stepdad like that, but what's the point of anything if you can't wind people up a bit?'

I don't answer.

'I've thought about what you said.' He laughs briefly although nothing is funny. 'Maybe I don't know anything, but I'd like to know more. I think your dad was impressive. I'd like you to tell me more.'

'Don't talk about my father,' I say sharply. 'You have no right to talk about him. He's not a topic of casual conversation.'

His face loses its humour. 'I'd never consider your father a topic of casual conversation.'

What do I do? I need my job and I can't let him wreck it for me. I sit beside him. Ollie does that sometimes when friends come in. It's a quiet time in the afternoon and I won't take long. 'Listen,' I say, my voice hushed, 'we've got nothing to say to each other. Your stepdad approached me because he's afraid you're going to join the Disciples or … who knows what? And he was hoping I could stop you. But he made a mistake. He's wrong. You can join the Disciples. You can jump off a cliff. You can do whatever you want because I don't care. It's got nothing to do with me. Now, just leave me alone.'

'You really are upset?' The idea seems to bemuse him.

'Justin, that is your name?' He nods. 'Stop coming in here.' I stand up.

'Wait.' He catches my arm. 'I … I know I say things I shouldn't. Stuff comes out my mouth when I should shut up but I would like to talk to you. Forget about Ian. I don't care what he wants. This isn't about him.'

Something in his voice stops me. I watch him closely.

'I read about your dad, and … my father was killed too. I know what that does to you. It fucks you up, so I'd just like to talk to you.'

His expression alters. I can see the vulnerability behind his veneer. I'm also aware other customers have turned to us; I've been standing there too long. Or worse, they're earwigging our conversation. I make a quick decision. I need to get Justin away from me.

'I'll meet you for half an hour after work, and then you leave me alone. You don't come in here again.'

His eyes momentarily brighten. 'Yeah.' He nods. 'That's okay. Let's … let's meet at the Quayside Arms.'

I know the pub. It's down by the Thames and far enough away from here. I nod and walk away.

CHAPTER 16

The Quayside Arms has an outdoor area that overlooks the Thames. Justin's sitting there. It isn't a warm evening so he's alone. He draws on a cigarette as I sit opposite him. He exhales, the smoke catching the breeze.

'Want one?' he offers.

I shake my head. He goes inside to get us both a half pint. I look out at the river and the boats moving along it. It feels safer being outside than inside. He comes back and sits down.

'Do you believe in justice?' he asks.

'Justice?'

'Yeah.' He raises his glass and takes a sip. 'I don't,' he says with conviction. 'I mean … I believe in it, as something that should exist, but I don't see much of it about.'

I don't reply.

'Your father … he didn't get justice,' he says.

'No,' I agree, aware of how careful I need to be. 'Nobody should be imprisoned like he was – not without being charged and put on trial.'

'My father didn't get any justice either.' His eyes hold mine.

'What happened to him?' I ask softly.

'He was killed in a car crash by some fucking idiot on their phone. A senseless fucking death and the guy didn't even get banged up. So like I said, there's no justice.'

'It doesn't sound like it.'

Justin draws on his cigarette, exhales and continues. 'I think I accept the world as it is. Sometimes I tell myself I'm alright, but really, I'm so fucking angry all the time. Don't you feel that?'

'Sometimes,' I say.

'But at least your dad had the Disciples on his side. That raid on Colchester House – it was inspired.' He smiles. 'God, I loved watching that clown Chief Inspector Bradley at his press conference, mouthing off about how successful they'd been in otherwise curtailing the Disciples. He had no idea it was coming.' He claps his hands, gleeful.

I feel rising panic – we're in a public space. 'Keep your voice down, Justin,' I hiss. 'And my father's dead, that's what that raid achieved.'

He's quiet, watching me. 'Why do you think he joined the Disciples?' This time, at least, he lowers his voice.

'I don't know that he did. All I know is what the media reported, and I don't believe that.'

'I'd agree with you there. Most of the shit you read is lies, but they busted him out of Colchester House so he *was* one of them. Even Ian couldn't lie to himself after that. He admired your dad too, but not for the reasons I do.'

'Why should you admire him?' I ask.

'Because I've been reading up about LifeStar Corporation,' he says. 'And it's clear as day they're part of the problem, not the solution. And "If you're not part of the solution, you're part of the problem, there's no in between."' He's quoting the Disciples, one of their mottos on the internet. He grins like he's said the cleverest thing. 'That's what your dad knew. Be honest.'

My chest feels tight, it's hard to breathe.

'I don't know what my father knew,' I say, but my voice doesn't sound strong. I have to change the subject. 'Anyway, what is it you're studying that you're so interested in this stuff?'

'Life. Injustice. The shit and lies we're told,' he says, 'and at university, maths. I'm good at maths. No, that's not true, I'm *very* good at maths. Computers too.'

'I never really liked maths,' I say, hoping desperately to keep him off the subject of my father. 'Music's my thing.'

He shrugs, uninterested. 'Do you like working in that coffee shop?'

'Liking it isn't the point. They pay me.'

'I wouldn't want to work in a coffee shop. Somebody at the top will be making loads of money and you're probably being paid shit. It all just feeds the one big capitalist system.'

'Not everybody's got the choices you have.'

'No,' he says casually.

'Your stepdad's got a lot of money,' I point out. 'That protects you, it gives you opportunities. I was once like that too. But the system's what it is. I don't imagine I can change it.'

'The Disciples might,' he says, and smiles.

'I don't know what the Disciples might do.' I can feel the sweat under my arms. 'But my father died with them, so they're not doing much good.'

'I'd contact them if I could,' he says very quietly. 'I was hoping you could help me do that.' His face is serious, his eyes cold. 'I reckon … you know how to do that.'

I feel the bile rise at the back of my throat. 'I don't know how you figure that out, Justin, but you're wrong. You couldn't be more wrong. I hate the Disciples. I've nothing to do with them.' I stand up to go. 'Please leave me alone now. We've got nothing else to say to each other.'

I leave the pub quickly, walking at speed away from him.

'Dominic,' he calls.

I start to run.

'Dominic!' He catches up.

I turn on him. 'Don't call me Dominic. I'm Luke. Stop harassing me.'

'Your father was a good man, Luke,' he says loudly. 'Maybe you don't want to see justice done, but I do.'

'Don't you tell me about my dad.' I'm shaking. 'He was my father, I'm the one who knew him. You talk about justice but you have no idea. If you really want to make a difference, ask your stepdad what it is he does all day.'

I run from him towards the Tube. It isn't my usual stop but I don't care. I race down the escalator. The train pulls in, I get on and the doors close behind me.

CHAPTER 17

I get home and clamber up the stairs to our flat. The door is ajar; that's not normal. I push it open carefully. Looking down the hallway, I know immediately something is wrong.

'Charley,' I call.

She appears in the doorway to the living room. 'We've been broken into.'

I go to her quickly and glance round at the mess. We don't have many possessions but what we do have has been ransacked. Cutlery is on the floor, cushions have been pulled from their covers, and every cupboard in the kitchen opened.

'Shit,' I mutter.

'I can't believe it,' Charley says, hoarse. 'It's as bad as when Dad was arrested.'

No, it's not as bad as that. Whoever's broken in here hasn't emptied bags of flour over the cooker, they haven't trashed the place, but still, it brings back the worst memories.

'My laptop's gone,' she says.

I feel my anger rising. 'They've probably taken everything they can sell quickly.'

'It makes me sick thinking of who's been through our things. Flint's not back yet, so there'll be stuff of his that's gone. I just haven't clocked it up yet.' She pauses, looking pale and small. 'You'd better check your room.'

I walk slowly into my bedroom. The mattress has been upturned, the chest of drawers opened and the box I hide under my bed, in the farthest corner, has been broken open. I check it quickly. They've taken the money I kept inside, but that's not what makes me freeze.

'Oh, God, no.' I tremble. It's hard to breathe. 'Charley, we're in trouble.'

I hear her approach behind me. My legs feel weak. 'The gun,' I whisper. 'It's gone.'

The blood begins to drain from my limbs. Everything is spiralling out of control. The gun, the gun Gil gave me, has gone. It names me a Disciple; I've wiped it clean but his fingerprints might still be on it, and mine. I push past my sister to the bathroom. My hands grip the side of the toilet and I vomit. I can't think straight, can't allow my mind to imagine what might happen now.

'They don't have it,' Charley says. She's standing in the doorway.

'What?' I shiver.

'I got rid of it ... when we first moved in.'

'You what?' I take a few deep breaths then slowly straighten up. 'I ... don't understand.' I shake my head.

She speaks quietly. 'There was nowhere to hide it properly and I knew it was a security risk.'

'Then where is it?'

'Somewhere in the Thames near Hammersmith Bridge.'

I look at her caught between relief and anger. 'Did you not think to discuss it with me first?'

She doesn't answer, and then we hear Flint arrive. 'What the ...'

We spend hours tidying up the mess. We aren't sure how the thieves got into the flat. Nothing seems broken as such, but we call out a locksmith to change the lock and secure the front door. It's the sense of violation that gets us most, more than what they've actually taken.

'I'd been feeling safe here and now I don't,' Charley says.

We sit down to eat. It's late and we're tired. Flint has to go to work soon, but I wish he was staying with us.

'These things happen,' he says matter-of-factly, but he's upset too. They've taken the tablet he recently bought and cash Rena gave him.

'At least we've still got our phones,' I say, although it doesn't feel much consolation. 'And they didn't take my sax.'

I glance across at the two photos from Dad's office, the Bible and the pen that still sit on the bookshelf. 'Although, I'm surprised they didn't take the pen. Who knows, it might be valuable.'

'Dom, do you really think the arseholes who took our stuff are selling pens to their mates?' Flint says, angry.

Charley's close to tears. 'All of it leaves me feeling dirty … horrible. They didn't take Dad's stuff but they went through my clothes. What did they think they'd find behind my underwear?'

'Jewellery, probably,' Flint says.

'Fat chance,' she mutters.

We are quiet for a while, each in our own misery.

Charley breaks the silence. 'At least they didn't get the gun. Who knows what they might have done if they had?' She turns to me slowly.

'You should have told me,' I say softly, although I'm glad she got rid of it.

Flint shrugs; he knew about it too.

'We did what we had to,' Charley says. 'You know yourself you were never going to let it go. You thought it provided some kind of protection, but it didn't.'

'I know but … it feels like you've been keeping a secret from me.' I look down at my plate, quiet; I've been keeping a secret too. I let out a long sigh. Why has it been such a shit day?

I look up slowly. 'Listen. There's something I have to tell

you.' I pause. 'Something else happened, and …' They're not going to like what I have to say. I tell them about Pendleton and Justin. 'I know you were right to get rid of that gun, but I just feel, no matter what I do … one way or another I can never escape the Disciples.'

Both Charley and Flint are silent. I can't tell if they're shocked or angry.

'Is there anything else you need to tell us?' Flint asks carefully.

'No, that's it, and I didn't tell you about Pendleton approaching me again because I didn't want you to worry. I thought I could get rid of him and that would be it.'

'What about his son, Justin, do you think you've seen the last of him?' Charley asks.

'I hope I've seen the last of him.' Yet I'm not sure.

'Because the Pendletons seem very persistent,' Charley says.

'Yes, but what do I do?'

'Leave Coffee Primo.' She's serious. 'Find work else-where in a completely different part of London. If you're not around, then whatever the Pendletons want, you're not there.'

'I don't want to do that,' I say slowly. I shiver, she means it. 'I haven't landed on my feet like you, Charley … there's no Jackson to help me out.'

'But it's the safest thing to do,' she says.

Flint speaks up. 'Wait a minute. Half our things have just been nicked and nobody's gonna make that better for us. Dom can't afford to leave his job. I don't like this guy Justin either, okay, he's a jerk. And him and his stepdad – there's something goin' on between them, but we can't let some jerk mess things up for us.'

'No,' I agree. 'And we need the money.'

Charley's still. 'I don't want you to have to leave your job.' She sighs. 'But I don't want him approaching you again.'

'No,' Flint says. 'But if he does, Dom keeps doin' what he always does – he lies.'

'Of course,' I say.

She's thoughtful. 'In a way it's not lying now. It's the truth because any evidence to prove otherwise is at the bottom of the Thames.'

At that, I almost feel relief.

I sit on my bed and pick up my notebook. Whoever broke into the flat left it untouched; it's no more use to a thief than the pen. I open it. Mary's feathers are still inside. I hold one in each hand. They're almost weightless. I close my eyes a moment and wonder what it would feel like to fly. To fly away from danger and pain. Although being able to fly didn't save the eagle. I open my eyes and the feathers blow up and across the room. I gaze quickly at the window; they've been caught in a breeze, but the window is shut … there is no breeze. I move to gather each one up. Is a feather something that is alive or dead? Inert or active? I think of the eagle they came from.

'*It doesn't know it's dead,*' a voice whispers in my head. '*It's forgotten it can't fly, so it thinks it is.*'

'Don't be crazy,' I say aloud, trying to still my own thoughts. I put the feathers back inside the book. On the next page is the eleven-digit mobile number. I stare at it a while, memorising it, yet still can't tear it out.

CHAPTER 18

Gregory opens the door to the cottage and we all step inside.

'A few people stayed here after you did,' Gregory says. 'But it needs some attention now.'

When Charley, Flint and I stayed in it, it needed attention, let alone now, but I don't say that.

'This place could be great,' Mary says, excited.

'Well … a lot better than it is,' Gregory agrees.

'I might live here a while.' She smiles. 'I've never lived on my own, and I'd like to see what it's like.'

I glance at Gregory. 'Don't you want the rent?'

He shrugs. 'I've not had any rent for ages. It's Mary's choice.'

I stand there, surprised at how all right I feel. When we first drove up, I felt anxious returning to somewhere that has such mixed memories for me.

'I can see it as your home, Mary,' I say. 'Maybe paint some of the walls a colour?' That would definitely change the atmosphere.

Gregory walks over to the fridge. 'Anyway, today we're getting rid of all these old appliances. You can help me put them in the back of the truck, and I'll take them to the dump.'

He disconnects the oven and pulls the plug on the fridge. I help him shift both of them through the small front doorway and into the pickup truck. He drives off and Mary and I go back inside. We walk up the stairs to check out the bedrooms.

'That bed,' I say, pointing to the one I slept in, 'was not comfortable. Neither was Flint's,' I say of the other. 'They should go to the dump too.'

'We'll not be sleeping in them,' she promises. 'I'll get a new one – king size.'

We walk into the other room; my sister slept in it.

'I like the view out the back.' I gaze out the window across the landscape to the mountains in the distance.

'Do you know what I'd like to do?' Mary says, her voice surprisingly soft.

'What?' I turn to her.

She walks over. She draws me away from the window and pushes me gently against the wall. Her lips touch mine. 'Guess,' she whispers. Then she kisses my neck at the top of my T-shirt and moves down my body. Her hands start to undo the belt on my jeans and lower the zip. I know exactly what she's going to do. I close my eyes and let her continue.

Afterwards, my mind is fuzzy with pleasure. I open my eyes and she's smiling.

'I've got you on my fingers,' she says, and runs her hand along the wall behind me. 'And now you've anointed the place.'

I laugh. 'This cottage will be good for you, Mary.'

We both grin. I look out the window again then we go downstairs and wait for Gregory.

Over dinner that night, we're relaxed with each other. I decide to speak about something at the back of my mind.

'Do you believe in ghosts?' I ask.

'Don't tell me, Dominic, you think the cottage is haunted.' Gregory shakes his head.

'Er … no, it hadn't crossed my mind.'

'I'm not saying nobody never died there,' he says, 'but it's certainly not haunted.'

'I really wasn't thinking of it,' I assure him. 'I was …' I pause. 'I was thinking of that eagle wing Mary has. You helped her preserve it.'

'Are you asking if it's haunted?' he asks, sceptical.

I shrug. 'I don't know. But what if … it doesn't know it's dead.'

'Doesn't know it's dead?' Gregory says, pointedly. 'Of course it doesn't know it's dead just like it doesn't know it's alive either. It's not conscious – it doesn't know anything.'

I turn to Mary. 'But what I mean is, does its *spirit* know it's dead?' What am I saying? I sound half mad.

She's thoughtful. 'I think its spirit is beyond life and death.'

'Have you two been at my whisky?' Gregory asks, incredulous. 'Or did you find some magic mushrooms in the back garden?'

Mary and I both laugh. I look down, embarrassed. 'I'm sorry. I've no idea what I'm on about.'

'No,' Gregory agrees. Then he turns to Mary. 'Don't encourage him, Mary. He can't handle it – whatever you've been telling him.'

There's a loud knock from outside, someone at the door to the shop. Gregory looks at his watch. 'Ah, that'll be Rosie.' He rises to go down and let her in. I hear his footsteps on the stairs, and then the bell tinkle as he opens the shop door.

'It's Aunt Rosie,' Mary informs me.

I hear them clumping up the stairs. Rosie bursts into the living room and looks around. Her gaze stops on me. She isn't exactly fat, but her body seems to take up a lot of space. Her long grey hair is tied up at the back, and her blue eyes are the colour of the sea.

'New sofa, Greg,' she announces.

'I've had it a while, you've just not noticed.'

'I'd have upcycled the old one for you, you just needed to ask.'

'I'd had it fifteen years, Rosie. I wanted a new one.'

She shakes her head slightly. I shift where I sit.

'You know, Dominic,' she says to me directly, even though we've not been introduced, 'I think they've been keeping me from you. It's not like I don't see my brother regularly nor indeed my niece, and you two have been going out for how long?' She shrugs and comes to sit at the table next to me.

'Why would we do that, Rosie?' Gregory asks, returning to his own chair.

'Scared the wee lad will be frightened off when he meets the larger family.'

Mary laughs.

Gregory says, 'Rosie, I've called Dominic many names over the years, but "wee lad" has never been one of them.'

She looks me up and down; there's no hiding she's summing me up. 'So, Dominic,' she says more gently, 'I take it you must love Mary very much considering you came back to her after all that time apart and you being in London.'

'I do,' I say.

'Well, that's good. You make her very happy. It's a wonderful thing if you can make another person that happy.' She smiles, but her eyes are sad.

'Cup of boiling water?' Gregory interjects before I can reply.

'Yes please, Gregory,' she says then turns back to me. 'I don't drink tea or coffee, too many air miles involved. An addiction we need to get over in the West if we want to look after the planet.'

I realise it is not the moment to tell her I work in a coffee shop.

'I bring my own herbs.' She rises to follow Gregory into the kitchen.

The room feels empty in her absence. I can hear her and Gregory mumbling in the kitchen.

'Rosie's a one-off,' Mary confides. 'Sometimes she can get a bit much, but mostly she's okay.'

'She speaks her mind,' I say.

'She's wanted to meet you for a long time … she's very protective of me.'

'So your dad trusts me enough now?'

Mary smiles coyly. 'Something like that. And he's figured you can take her. She's … she's a good person, deep down. Some tough things have happened to her so she can seem a bit hard, but deep inside she's got a lot of love to give.'

I look at Mary and realise she only sees the best in people.

'I love you,' I say, because I know I'm not as good.

I lie in bed aware of a sadness sitting in my chest; I go back to London tomorrow. Mary's body is curved into mine. Holding her, I drift into sleep.

I am going down the escalator to the Tube. It's a weekday, rush hour. Heads gaze into phones, a closed umbrella drips water, and the woman in front of me is carrying bags of shopping. Everything is familiar, the usual rush of people trying to get home from work. I stare ahead as the escalator nears the bottom. Then I see him, turning down a corridor towards the platform. It doesn't make sense. It can't be him, not taking the Tube, not with the endless cameras watching. Yet … I have to follow. I want to run but the woman in front of me is waddling away. I move quickly round her and race towards the Tube. I feel the sudden rush of air, warm and clammy, as the train comes in. My eyes search to the right, the left.

The doors to the train open. Passengers get off. I think I can see him further down. He doesn't look around and I can't call his name. I try to push my way through the mass of passengers exiting, but he gets on. I'm not fast enough. The doors close. The brakes release with a hiss and the train moves slowly forward, disappearing carriage by carriage into the tunnel. I watch him pass by, but he's looking down so he doesn't see me. He vanishes, his name repeating in my head with the rhythm of the wheels on the track. Gil. Gil. Gil. It fades to silence.

Opening my eyes, I'm disorientated. I'm lying in my small bed in London only then I realise I'm not. I'm with Mary. It was a dream. I feel another sadness, but won't admit it.

CHAPTER 19

Justin Pendleton walks into Coffee Primo. I guess I always knew he'd come back. It doesn't matter that I don't want to see him; the Pendletons have their own rules of engagement. He orders his usual drink and panini. I take the toasted sandwich to him.

'You'll want to speak to me when you've read this.' He puts an envelope on the table and slides it towards me.

I don't reply and I don't pick it up.

'I found it on Ian's computer,' he says. 'My way of asking: what does he do all day?' He grins mischievously.

I tell myself to walk away, to have nothing to do with it.

He lowers his voice. 'It's proof of just how bad LifeStar Corporation is.'

I freeze. I know I must turn away, now. It's imperative; I cannot get involved. But another part of me stretches out my hand and picks up the envelope.

I read it at home sitting on my bed. I read it once, twice and then I turn the paper over and back again, checking the words don't disappear, because I'm struggling to believe what I'm reading. I'm holding a letter written on paper with the official LifeStar Corporation heading. It's typed and produced in Ian's name. It's marked as having been distributed to three people, two of whom are in the Ministry of Defence. My breath quickens. This is it. I'm holding solid proof that LifeStar Corporation and the military are working together. It states Operation Olethros is advancing. Stage One is near completion. Stage Two will commence shortly: the Kendrick facility is ready, and the piece of vital information they've been waiting for is within reach.

My hands shake. Does Justin have any idea what this relates to? Or what he's done and what the consequences might be? He's written his mobile number at the top of the letter. I ring it. I don't care what I agreed with Charley and Flint, I have to make contact. This is too important. He picks up quickly.

'Justin.' My voice is tight. 'Where are you?' I need to speak to him in private.

'Hey,' he says, upbeat. 'Glad you called. I'm sitting in my bedroom reading a textbook. It's so boring I'm not sure how to stay awake.'

'Where did you get this?' I demand.

'I told you, off Ian's computer.'

I take a deep breath. He sounds relaxed, breezy; he has no idea. For a few seconds I consider what to say, given the possibility somebody could be listening in, or some spy software might be triggered by certain keywords. I speak slowly.

'The company your father works for has a monitoring system whereby everything saved and taken from the organisation is recorded and traced. Possibly, everything that's printed is monitored too. The letter you've ... it's confidential, highly confidential, so you have no idea what chain reaction you may have just set in motion.'

He laughs. 'I disabled that.'

'What?' My head's spinning.

'I'm not sure I'd call it a monitoring system, not as such, it's more like an index. But I figured how to switch it off, at least while I printed.'

'You disabled their system?' I whisper. 'How can you be sure?'

He laughs again. 'The fact you've got to ask that is proof

you'd not understand the explanation. I told you I was good with computers and I wasn't going to let something like that stop me.' There is a pause. 'Maybe now you understand how serious I am.'

I close my eyes. Yes, he's serious.

'Did you … did you find anything else?' I ask, and then add quickly, 'No, don't tell me. Not on the phone. We need to meet.'

'Of course,' he says. 'I'm busy the next few days but free Friday. How about I pick you up after work?'

'We'll need to go somewhere private.'

'Yeah, I'll have the car. We'll take a drive. There'll just be you and me.'

I'm not sure I like that idea but I can't think of anything else. 'Okay. Friday. Meet me after work.'

'Great.'

He hangs up. I look down at my phone. What have I done? He's got my number now. He told me he disabled LifeStar's system on his father's computer. He's shown me a letter that feels like dynamite. I'm reeling. Dad spent years in prison for trying to get out information like this. Am I on the verge of achieving something I'd thought impossible? Has the right person with the right information come along at the right moment for something to finally come to fruition?

What if Justin can access other documents? I could get them to Gil. I might even be able to leak them myself. I feel a rush of excitement and terror. I can hear Charley and Flint in the kitchen. We'll eat dinner soon but I have to think through what to do.

Charley laughs, and I make an immediate decision. I won't tell her or Flint what's happened. Not now. I'll wait until I know more. If I tell them now, if I show them the letter, they'll want me to stop. I can't stop, not when I'm this close.

I walk slowly into the living room. Flint is chopping vegetables and Charley's dipping them in hummus.

'Want some?' she calls over.

'Yeah,' I say, and carry on as though everything is normal.

What do I do? My thoughts keep churning. And what about the Disciples? Should I tell Justin I can make contact with them? It's what he's wanted and they're the obvious people to give the information to. But if I do tell Justin, what other questions might he ask?

I get out of the shower and stare at my reflection in the mirror, as though somehow it can answer the question. The bullet wound in my shoulder is still a significant scar, it will never go away.

Mary kissed it once, very gently. 'You got hurt,' she said.

'Yes,' I answered.

Her eyes held mine. And she could've asked me how it happened or said she knew what it was, but she didn't. Instead, she said, 'I love you.'

'Yes,' I whispered, glad for what we didn't need to say.

But that doesn't alter the truth. I committed a crime; I blew up an oil pipeline. If the police ever get hold of me they won't care that I didn't want to do it, nobody will. Instead, they'll lock me up for years. I suddenly feel faint.

I sit quickly on the toilet and rest my head between my knees. I can never tell Justin about the Disciples. I break out in a sweat. How do I walk around every day forgetting I can be put in jail for years? I do it by pretending I'm somebody else, by believing the Disciples are people, an organisation, separate from me because I can't bear the truth: *I am* a Disciple. Dad was too. Gil said they'd avenge his death, but I've seen no evidence of that. I feel hot and confused.

I lean over the sink and splash cold water on my face, letting it run over my hands. I have to calm down. I'm not one of them. Gil used me. As Flint put it at the time, he groomed me. I think of the quote my father highlighted in the Bible: "and they shall beat their swords into plough-shares, and their spears into pruning hooks."

I understand what I must do. I will act alone. No violence. No Disciples.

CHAPTER 20

A red and black Mini pulls up at the kerb.

'Hey, Luke.' Justin opens the passenger door. The road is busy, the traffic backing up behind him. I jump in and we drive off.

'Good to see you.' He smiles.

I put on my seat belt. 'Yeah, well, we need to talk.' We're weaving through busy roads. 'Where we heading?'

'I've got this place I'm taking us to. You'll like it, it's private. Just outside London.'

'We don't need to go that far, do we?' I hadn't anticipated this. If I need to get away, how am I going to get back?

'Listen, Luke, I found us something important. You want to talk about it so can you at least trust me a little?' He glances over and shrugs his shoulders.

'I can try,' I say honestly. 'I don't always find it easy to trust people. Not given everything that's happened.'

'If you don't mind me saying I think you worry too much,' he says plainly. 'I read that stuff online about how they were looking for you – but that was years ago. I mean, who's interested in you now your father's dead? And why not call yourself Dominic?'

For a moment I almost hit him. He has no idea: not about what Dad did to us or what happened with the Disciples. How would he live with those things? I feel such rage my skin prickles. But then, of course he has no idea: I've told him nothing. And I need to keep hold of the fact he found that letter.

I struggle to speak then calm myself. 'I just got used to being Luke.'

'Well, all I'm saying is I think it will help you if you can start to think of me as a friend.'

'Okay,' I say slowly.

We drive a while in silence.

'What do you do when you're not working in that coffee shop?' Justin asks.

'Do?' I say. 'Well, um, I like to play the sax. If I've got enough money I'll go to a gig. Like I said, music's my thing, I focus on that.'

'Hmm. I like working out. I spend a lot of time at the gym.' He takes his hand off the gear stick and flexes his arm muscle proudly.

'I'm not that into sport or working out,' I say.

'You should be, it helps with girls, and ... I mean you always feel better if you're strong, don't you?'

I shrug, maybe.

'You got a girlfriend?' he asks.

'Not at the moment.'

'Then you should definitely start working out,' he says jovially.

'Girls like different things,' I say softly.

'I don't have a girlfriend,' he tells me. 'I love sex, so don't get me wrong, I've had loads of sex, but a girlfriend – I don't think they're worth it. They always want something, don't they? Emotionally.'

'Well, I guess if you love someone there's give and take.'

'I don't believe in love,' he states flatly. 'It's like justice, a great concept but I don't see much of it about, not really.'

I watch him: his blue eyes fixed on the road, his light brown hair growing longer, stubble on his chin. He's hard to make out.

'What about your folks?' I ask. 'Don't you think they love each other?'

'Puh.' He rolls his eyes.

'Do you love them?'

He's quiet for a moment, thinking. 'Mum's cool. She's great, I guess I love her. We get on.'

'And Ian?' I ask carefully.

'Ian.' He lets out a sigh. 'He tries so hard to be my friend, but he's not my father and he's not my friend. Mostly, I like winding him up. Right now, my smoking really gets to him. Sometimes I'll smoke in the living room just to have the smell stick to those curtains he cares about so much.' He laughs briefly, but I don't think he's happy.

We are quiet for a while. We reach the outskirts of London and he hits the accelerator. I hope we're not going much further. I half listen as Justin chats on, boasting about his abilities on the computer and in the gym. At last, he pulls off the main road and we make our way down a rough-surfaced lane. He stops the car and gets out. I follow him and we walk to a clearing. I'm looking out over a small lake. I'd no idea such a place existed, and we're not even far from London. The evening air is warm and the water is calm, almost motionless. Trees flank us, and there's no one else around. It's definitely private.

'You a good swimmer?' Justin asks.

'I'm an okay swimmer.'

He turns to me and smiles. 'Then let's go in. I love wild swimming.'

'Wild swimming?' I hadn't bargained on this.

'Yeah, you've got to be careful when you get in, you'll feel the roots of trees beneath your feet, and the reeds and grasses lapping at your legs, and it's so cold you'll think you're dying but then you pass this threshold and the cold feels good.'

'Justin, we just need to talk.'

'And the best part is,' he says, 'look around, there's not

another person in sight. You can drown if you don't know what you're doing, and there's no one here to rescue you.' He chuckles. Something about that possibility excites him.

I'm silent. How do I handle him? This is not what I want at all.

'Come swimming with me and then … I'll consider you a friend.' He smiles slyly. 'And I'll share what I know.'

'Justin, I've not got a towel or trunks with me, so you swim and then we'll talk. I'm still a friend.'

He laughs. 'Who wears trunks? We're going in naked, man. Then you drip dry.'

Oh, shit. What do I do? But before I can say anything else he's stripping off his clothes, he doesn't hesitate. His skin is pale, his body slim and muscular; he definitely works out. I watch him enter the water carefully. He gasps at the cold, then pushes off from the side.

'Get in,' he calls over. 'You'll love it.'

'I won't love it. I'll wait here.'

'Come on, Luke. What you scared of?'

'I'm not scared of anything, I'm just not getting in that water.'

'Don't be such a girl … or is that it? You're going to strip off and I'm going to see you're a girl. Ian said things like that can happen – genetically – to people.'

That's it, he's managed to wind me up. I've swum with more strength and for a longer distance than he ever will. I finally strip off. I don't want him gazing at my body so I dive quickly into the water, completely ignoring the fact I should get in carefully, because I'm not afraid of drowning. I go under, scrape the bottom and then rise.

'Jesus, it's cold.' My teeth start chattering. It's freezing but I've experienced worse.

He laughs. 'If you swim hard and quick, you adjust. You start to heat up.'

We swim side by side. I watch our clothes, discarded

on the grass verge, disappear behind us. A dog might pick them up then they won't be there when we return. I keep a steady pace, aware I could race ahead, but I don't want him to know I swim that well. He speeds up and I increase my pace too. He goes faster again, challenging me, and still I keep up. Then he dives down under the water and starts to push ahead. I join him; I may not be as fit but I'm not going to let him get that far ahead of me. And then I almost make a mistake. My lungs are empty of air; he hasn't risen, and I can just get past him if I stay down longer. I start to take the smallest breath underwater. I can't do that. Nobody can ever know what I'm capable of. I hit the bottom hard with my feet and break the water's surface. I cough and splutter, readjusting. He rises twenty metres ahead.

'Beat you,' he says triumphantly.

I'm struggling to catch my breath.

'Don't drown.' He laughs.

My breathing calms. I make one last cough and then I'm okay. 'You beat me,' I concede.

He grins, pleased with himself. We continue swimming keeping a steady pace. The cold feels less cold. The trees at the side cast their shadows on the water and the sun glistens on its surface. I suddenly realise how special it is swimming like this with nobody else around, just trees and birds singing and the evening sun sinking slowly in the sky. For some reason I think of Gil; he might swim like this too.

'We should probably head back,' Justin says, turning around.

I flip over and look up. I kick my legs a while, heading slowly to where we started. Then we both finish doing the front crawl.

I get out the water and feel the air on my skin. I shake myself as dry as I can before hastily putting on my clothes. My T-shirt goes on first. I can't risk him commenting on the scar on my shoulder. Dressed, I turn to him. He's only put his jeans on and is sitting with his face towards the setting sun, his eyes closed. I shiver, cold, but he doesn't seem bothered. He's peaceful. I'm glad he brought me here and I don't reckon he's often peaceful. Eventually, he gets up and puts on the rest of his clothes. We walk back to the car and get inside.

'That was good,' he says, sounding relaxed.

'Yeah,' I agree.

'Maybe you'll go wild swimming again.'

'Who knows? But yeah, I liked it.'

I can feel my muscles like I haven't felt them for a long time. The sun has almost completely set. Justin's got access to some of the most important information I'm ever likely to see, and I swam with him because that's what he wanted. Now it's my turn.

I speak in a hushed voice. 'What else did you find on Ian's computer?'

'Nothing. I could only access that single letter. I guess he'd been working on it and everything else he'd left at work.'

I'm disappointed yet say nothing.

'But I think that letter's important,' he says.

'Yes.' I turn to him. 'It's very important.' Am I ready to take the leap, to take the risk of my life?

CHAPTER 21

'Justin, there's something I want to tell you, but I need to know I can trust you.' I pause. 'I mean *really* trust you and, right now, I don't know you well enough to know if I can do that.'

He is quiet and serious. 'Okay,' he says slowly. 'Well, you can trust me. I know I've ... I've wound you up, but I like you. I definitely like you.'

'That's not enough,' I say.

He stalls, thinking. 'Is ... is this about the Disciples? I kind of guessed you're involved with them.'

'Wrong, Justin. You're about to completely blow it. I have nothing to do with the Disciples.'

'Well, will it help then if I say I won't mention them again?'

'It will be essential. It means you get it – I have nothing to do with them.'

We're both quiet. The penny's dropped; he understands how serious I am. He sits back, contemplative.

'Okay.' He takes a deep breath. 'I'm going to tell you something that ... I find pretty difficult ... like on a personal level.'

I wait, listening.

He speaks in a soft voice. 'When I was fourteen, I used to go into Ian's study and log on to his computer. He had no idea I could do that. And ... I tried to hack into systems like the army, and a couple of banks. I even considered the Pentagon.' He pauses. I'm silent. 'It was just a challenge, you know, to see if I could do it. It wasn't like I wanted to do anything with the information I accessed.' I watch him closely. His face twitches slightly. 'So one Sunday I managed to get into the Met Police's criminal database. It was a fluke. I remember my hands shaking because I couldn't believe I'd done it. I scanned through some documents. I didn't change them or tamper with anything, I was just enjoying the fact I'd breached their security system. Then I came out of it all, logged out of his computer and thought that was the end of it.' He shakes his head gently. 'Shit, was I naïve,' he says bitterly. I wait for him to continue.

'So later, this police car pulls up and two officers want to interview Ian. Their system picked up the breach. I hadn't realised it could do that. And suddenly, they're threatening me with a prison sentence. Ian phoned up some lawyer friend, and the police took me in and put me a cell. Because I was only fourteen they weren't meant to interview me until Ian and the lawyer arrived but they took the opportunity to strip-search me and ... you know, humiliate me. And then later ... I don't quite know how Ian did it, but he bought the police off. They came to some arrangement. I had to show them exactly what I'd done. And at home, I was grounded for six months. I didn't get any pocket money and I was sent to a psychiatrist for weeks. But the worst thing was Mum crying. For days, every time I walked into a room with her she burst into tears. The psychiatrist told me that my actions had been a trauma to her, and reopened the trauma of Dad's death.' He's breathing hard. He shivers. 'They made me feel like shit.'

I listen, stunned. I had no idea he could do such a thing. I can also hear the anger and pain in his voice.

He turns to me. 'But what it taught me is this,' he says with determination. 'The police are bastards. I'm not going to tell you what else they did to me in that cell, alone, but if I'd had the guts to tell anyone …' He shakes his head again, his lower lip trembling. Then after a while he continues, his voice stronger. 'It taught me there is always a monitoring system somewhere. I knew exactly what I had to look for before I printed off that LifeStar letter.' He stops.

I don't say anything, trying to take it all in.

Suddenly, he opens the car door and gets out. He goes to stand by the lake, silent. I follow slowly. I know what it is to do something wrong and how you can never take it back; maybe Justin feels like that too. It's messed him up, like his father's death, that's what I can see. I have a sudden, intense desire to tell him about the Disciples, and what I've done and how Gil messed me up. It would be a relief to get it off my chest, to tell someone who might understand. But I stop myself. I don't, I know I can't tell anyone.

'Nothing's ever what it seems,' he says slowly, his voice bitter.

'No,' I agree.

Then he turns to me. 'Have I wasted my time telling you my secret? Hey, Luke. Humiliating myself?'

'No,' I say softly. 'I'm glad you told me. I get you more now.'

He half smiles. 'And don't imagine Ian approached you because he cares about me. I embarrass him. He likes to get other people to sort me out.'

'Well,' I say, 'he made a mistake there.'

Justin is still.

It's a while before I can continue. I take a deep breath, then whisper, 'Before my father was arrested … he told me something so powerful and important I've never been able to share it with anyone, except with my sister at the time.'

Justin's alert, listening.

'He told me about the project he was working on with LifeStar Corporation. A project that involved LifeStar in collaboration with the Ministry of Defence making a … weapon of mass destruction, a genetic weapon that can be targeted at specific ethnic groups. In a war situation, it could wipe people out but leave the physical structures around them standing, intact, ready – as Dad put it – for immediate occupation.' Does that sound real? Even though I know it's true, it's still hard to believe.

'Dad knew it was terrible, evil, so he risked everything to try and reveal that information, to whistle-blow on LifeStar. But he never managed to do it. And the Disciples were no help. But now, that letter you showed me, I think it relates to that project. The one he was, and now Ian is, working on.'

The air feels close. A dragonfly hovers over the water.

'That's heavy shit,' Justin says slowly. His face is pale, shocked. 'It's … I could never have imagined that.'

'No,' I say. 'It's not something you can imagine.'

'Were you afraid when he told you?'

'Of course,' I say. 'Terrified. I didn't want to believe it. I begged him to leave LifeStar, to get another job, to not get involved. I knew the police and MI5 would go after him.'

'Jesus,' he says, letting out a long breath. 'So that's what Project Olethros is?

'It has to be. If there was just some other evidence to prove it … I'd be willing to leak that information on the web, send it to papers, and let the world know what's going on. I'd finish what my father couldn't do. Justice would finally be done.' I stop. There, I've said it all, out loud.

Justin holds my gaze. 'I'm glad you told me.'

'Yes, and you've wanted to join the Disciples, but hope-fully you realise they're not the point. We could … make a difference without them.'

He is quiet.

'But of course, now you understand what really happened to my father, you may not want anything to do with it.'

He shakes his head. 'Quite the opposite. There's a moral imperative to do something. We've got to get that evidence.'

I feel a strange mix of relief and anxiety; he's onside.

'I think the only way is to get other documents off their system,' I say. 'The letter you showed me, alone, it won't be enough.'

'I need to keep checking Ian's computer.'

'But if he doesn't bring home anything else that's relevant?' I ask.

'Then we may need to take more drastic action, but first, we'll watch what he does.'

I nod. 'But you realise, Justin, that there will be consequences for Ian if we succeed. Just like when the police turned up at your door. It will affect your mother.'

'Mum and I will be fine,' he says with steely determination. 'We were before Ian came along and we will be after him. But what we're talking about is bigger than Ian, or even your dad or the consequences we'll face. What they're doing goes against humanity, and a price needs to be paid. Justice must be done and I'm not afraid of that. I've been prepared to join the Disciples, Luke, which is not something you've managed. I do believe in what they stand for, but I'm happy to act with you alone. Really, we're all travelling to the same destination.'

In that moment, I realise he could be a Disciple; he has their determination and drive. His face is calm but serious. 'So we're agreed?' He puts out his hand.

'Yes,' I say, and we shake on it.

I get back late. Charley and Flint are in bed. That's a relief. I don't have to explain why I look like I've fallen in a river. Tomorrow, I'll tell them I went to a pub to hear a band. I'll also put some extra effort into practising the sax. I need everything to look as normal as possible.

I hate lying to them but they won't want me involved with Justin, or in what we're planning. They'll insist it's not safe. I can't pretend it isn't dangerous, but it's an opportunity I have to take.

CHAPTER 22

It's been the hottest day. The air is close and my room feels claustrophobic. I'm lying on my bed looking at the beads of water on my naked body. I took a cold shower but I'm still boiling. My phone rings. I lean over and pick it up.

'Hey.' It's Justin, he sounds happy. 'How's it going?' It's almost two weeks since we met.

'I'm good, but hot. Very hot.'

'Yeah, it's a good night for swimming.' Then he says conspiratorially, 'And a good night for gold-diggers … some nuggets have come up.'

'What do you mean?'

'Ian wants you to come round and join us for Sunday lunch.'

'What?' I sit up quickly.

'He's so glad we met up.' Justin chuckles. 'He thinks you're a good influence on me.'

'No way,' I say under my breath.

He drops his voice to a whisper. 'I've got something to show you, but you need to see it on his computer. Come round Sunday, and after lunch, he won't mind that we disappear upstairs. He won't have a clue.'

My shoulders tense; this is all becoming very real.

'Maybe we should pause and think this through,' I say.

'The thing with you, Luke, is you worry too much. I'm telling you, you'll want to see this. I thought you were brave.'

'Ian has no idea what we're doing, and I'm expected to turn up and eat lunch with you. There's only so much I can fake.'

'You'll be fine. You're a great fake.' He chuckles again.

'I'm not comfortable with this.'

'Then get over it, okay. Because you're the one who told me what he's working on, and that *cannot* continue.'

I'm quiet; he's right.

'Stay focused,' he insists. 'Keep cool and I'll see you at twelve.'

He hangs up, the call over. I stare out the window at the block of flats opposite. What has just happened? I'm going to lunch at the Pendletons. Justin has something to show me. What I've wanted is coming to fruition. I should be happy or feel some kind of positive emotion, but instead a dark cavity is opening up inside me. I've felt it before, like I'm drowning.

Later, it takes me a long time to fall asleep, then I dream.

I am alone in Mary's room. It's evening, and she's taking a bath. It's dark outside, winter. I pull out her desk chair and stand on it. I need to see the eagle wing again. I know she told me not to touch it, it's powerful, but right now I can't resist it. I pick it up, surprised at how light it is. My hand runs across the feathers. They're stiff with whatever preservative Gregory used on them.

'Nothing kills a top predator like an eagle,' I whisper, repeating Mary's words, 'except for human beings.'

I notice something begin to ooze from it, seeping out between the feathers. At first, it's a dark brown liquid, but then it brightens into red. I feel it warm on my fingers like blood. It is blood. The blood doesn't stop and the wing keeps oozing until it's running down my wrists. My left arm aches like it's being pulled at the shoulder, and the bullet wound burns. The pain of both intensifies, it becomes excruciating. And then ... I'm holding the wing but my left arm's attached to it, it's fused with the wing. It's no longer part of my body; it's come away from my shoulder … I'm tearing in two, ripping apart. I start screaming.

I wake and rush to feel my left arm. It's still there attached to my body. But the dream was so real I'm not sure. I scream again, the effort bringing me back to myself. The world comes into focus: my small room, the fuzz of darkness, the window open because it's stifling. There is a knock at the door.

'Dominic?' Charley opens it.

'I'm alright,' I say, breathy, 'I think.'

She comes in and sits on the edge of my bed.

'It was a bad dream just … the most horrible dream.' I shake my head, trying to shake it from my mind.

'I'm worried about you,' she says softly.

'No, I'm okay.' I don't sound it.

'You seem so closed these days.' Then she whispers into my head, *'I don't know what you're thinking, and I want to know that you're alright.'*

I feel hot and ashamed. 'I'm alright,' I say, aloud. Then continue into her head, *'We don't have to share everything about our lives, do we?'*

'No,' she agrees. *'But I sense there's something you're keeping from us and … I don't like that. You can tell me, you know.'*

I shake my head.

'Is it about Mary?' she asks.

'No. Things are good with Mary.'

'Then what is it?'

I swallow hard but can't answer.

'Did … did Justin approach you again?'

I don't want to lie and I can't tell the truth. 'I had a bad dream, Charley. That's all.'

'Then tell me about it,' she says gently. 'Please, Dom. I know something's bothering you.'

And I almost tell her, everything. I feel confused; I'm

losing control. 'I'm sorry I woke you,' I say instead. 'I can't tell you a dream, Charley, because I know what you're like.' I smile softly, my thoughts clearing. 'You think they hold some truth, but not this one. I can see that.'

She pauses; I'm not going to share it. 'I find it hard to sleep anyway,' she says, 'when it's this hot.'

'Yeah.'

'I'm going to the kitchen to get a drink, want to join me?'

'No, thanks. I just want to get some sleep.'

She leaves my room.

I lie back on my bed, but I daren't shut my eyes. I don't want to see that image in my mind again – my arm severed from my body. I peer through the gap in my curtains at the block across the way. I think of Mary sleeping in her room, and I know the dream isn't about her. In the silence, deep down, I understand the truth.

Saturday evening, I text Justin: 'Sorry can't make it tomorrow change of plan.'

His reply is swift. 'Don't bottle it now I've found what you want.'

CHAPTER 23

Sunday morning. Sun streams into the living room. It's another bright, summer's day. Lying back on the sofa, I watch Charley and Flint pack for a picnic.

'Are you sure you don't want to come?' Charley glances across at me. They're off to the park. 'There's a band playing later.'

'I don't feel great.' I haven't slept well and I'm finding it hard to pretend everything's all right. 'You go. I can always join you later. I just want to get more sleep.'

Flint finishes filling the bag with salad, bread and dips. 'Yeah, join us later.'

They head out. The flat is silent. My brain aches with the possibilities of the day. Do I go to the Pendletons'? Do I turn up and have lunch with them even though every part of me knows I might be facing a danger I can't fathom? I sense it but can't describe it. But what if Justin has the documents I want? Then the achievement will be immense.

'Go home and get on with your small, ordinary life.' Gil's words turn in my head. I've thought about them a lot since that terrible dream. There was a time when Gil tried everything possible to convince me to join the Disciples. Not now. Yet I'm not prepared to live a small, ordinary life.

I sit still and quiet, waiting for my fear to subside. Eventually, I'm calm. Justin will either have the evidence we need to expose LifeStar, or he won't. And if I can't trust him, if he pushes me too far, I'll back out and tell him we must never meet again. Then the last thing I'll do for my father will be to pass the letter on to the Disciples; I'll give Gil that. I'll have done my part. Today, I still have choices. I'm in control.

I shower and dress then sit on my bed. I think of the gun that was hidden beneath it. The one time I want it deep in my jacket pocket, and it's gone. Then I remember my father's pen sitting on the bookshelf. I pick it up. It's weightless compared to a gun but it feels like a talisman in my hand. The metal is cool and smooth. My trousers have an outside pocket halfway down the leg. I open it and slip the pen inside. It can't be seen, I can barely feel it, but it's there. I pick up my jacket and leave the flat quickly. I only have so much nerve.

Justin opens the front door. He looks relaxed in jeans and a T-shirt; there's a vintage album cover on it. His face broadens with a smile.

'Hey, you're here.' He pulls back the door to let me in. 'They're all in the garden. Ian's firing up the barbecue – which means we won't be eating any time soon.' He laughs. 'Come up to my room a while.'

I follow him into the hallway and then up the stairs to his room. It's a disorganised mess, a complete contrast to the rest of his parents' house. His duvet hangs off his bed, and his desk and the floor are scattered with books and papers. I see reams of what look like mathematical formulas. There are photos on the wall of him with a woman, I presume it's his mother, and a publicity poster for an old black-and-white movie.

'*The Third Man*,' I read.

'Yeah, I love film noir.'

'Okay,' I say, although I don't know the film.

'Nothing appears to be what it is, everyone's betraying one another, and there's a high body count. Just great.'

Above his desk is a printout from the internet: a grainy image of Gil Zimmerman caught on a security camera, his face in shadow, his right hand raised in the victory sign. It's an iconic image of him, his hand in the victory sign.

Justin watches me looking at it.

I shake my head. 'Is that to wind Ian up?'

'Of course,' he says, amused.

Our eyes meet and he's pleased. I can see how happy he is I'm there with him.

'Anyway,' he says, 'what we're doing beats Gil Zimmerman.'

I swallow hard. 'Keep your voice down and ... don't mention him.'

Again, he smiles.

'You said you've got something to show me,' I whisper.

'Later.' He nods. 'After lunch. They're drinking wine and beer out there. The longer the day goes on, the more they'll chill. And then they won't be paying any attention to us.'

'They?' I ask.

'Oh, yeah, Ian gets sociable when he's doing a barbecue. We've got Bill Grange here – a member of Ian's team, another geneticist. He's brought his wife. There's Mum's friend Greta, she's an artist. Anton Levinsky who's Ian's protégé in the office, and his girlfriend Sasha Simenoff. I've no idea what she's doing with him. Personally, I'd shag her senseless if I could. I'd give her a much better time than Anton.'

I'm shocked. 'You didn't tell me there would be people here from LifeStar.'

He shrugs. 'I didn't know until they turned up. Anyway, what does it matter? Just be glad Fiona Crane couldn't make it. She's the worst. I actually think it's funny, ironic, at least. And it doesn't change anything.'

'No?' I say sharply. 'They might have known my father – they probably did. What if they figure out who I am? Ian did.'

'Luke, chill. Your worrying is a serious problem. If you don't mind me saying, you need to deal with it. Nobody's interested in you – when are you going to get that? So what if you're Brian Minster's son? It's irrelevant now. You're here as my friend. Okay, *Luke?*' His eyes bore into me. 'They probably won't even bother to talk to you. They usually ignore me.' Then he adds, 'No, that's not true. Greta will talk to you. She talks to everybody. Stick by Greta if it bothers you.'

We go downstairs and I follow Justin into their large marble-topped kitchen. Packets of rolls and salads are laid out on the surface. There are cans of beer and bottles of wine. It all looks like you might expect. There is a burst of laughter from outside, male voices. I slow, hesitating. I might be making the biggest mistake. Some part of me knows I am. I should excuse myself now and leave, it's not too late. The roof of my mouth itches. If I go into that garden there'll be no turning back; my father's team will see me.

The French doors are open and Justin walks outside. I follow like I'm walking in a dream. The sunlight is blinding. I quickly put on my sunglasses; if only I'd gone for a larger design they'd cover more of my face. I'm standing in the Pendletons' landscaped garden. It's as stylish and expensive-looking as their home. There are two tiers of attractive-looking flower beds and stone shingle. The patio beneath me is black tiles and Ian is turning burgers and chicken on the huge gas-fired barbecue.

'Luke,' he calls over. 'Welcome.'

Everyone turns to Justin and me. I feel a rush of adrenalin.

'Meet Bill,' Ian says, and Bill steps forward to shake my hand. He pats Justin on the back. Bill has a dark brown beard and moustache; he appears much more like a scientist than Ian, he's even a little like Dad.

'And Joyce, Bill's wife and author of the children's book series "The Great and Gifted".'

She smiles politely. She reminds me of a teacher, serious and unadorned.

'And Greta,' Ian says, indicating a woman who's wearing a long tie-dyed dress that billows out.

Mrs Pendleton introduces herself. 'And I'm Martha.' Despite the heat she is smartly dressed in a loose-fitting blouse and flowing skirt. She has an unusual necklace of big colourful beads around her neck. Although she's Justin's mother, I can't see any resemblance between them. He must look like his father.

A couple at the bottom of the garden turn and walk towards us.

'Don't forget us,' the man says. He's wearing a dark blue top and beige shorts; he's younger than the rest.

'Anton,' Ian motions to him, 'and Sasha.'

Sasha flicks back her long red hair and smiles. I almost gasp, my heart pounding. It's Chloe, a Disciple we lived with in the Highlands. She was one of the few women there with long hair but it's the gap between her front teeth I'll never forget. I only ever saw her in grubby jeans and khaki fatigues but now she's wearing a short brightly coloured dress. It's cut low at the chest and sits high above her knees; it's definitely sexy. Anton smiles as my eyes linger on her, but only because he doesn't understand. He draws her closer to him proudly. But I don't fancy her, I'm freaking out. The world has stopped making sense.

'I love the azaleas at the back, Ian,' Sasha says sweetly, ignoring me. The voice is Chloe's. I don't know where to look.

'Do you want a beer or wine?' Justin asks.

'Something soft I think. A coke, thanks.' I can barely hold my voice steady. I can't drink alcohol. I have to stay sharp as a knife.

'Seriously?' Justin asks.

'Yeah, I'm thirsty,' I say, 'maybe have a beer later.' I feel rising panic. I'm in a garden with three members of my father's team from LifeStar Corporation and one Disciple. Or is Chloe still a Disciple? I know things change. Gemma's had a baby so is it possible Chloe's left them? Is this some new life she's invented for herself? Justin passes me a coke and I stand near a bowl of crisps. I keep my eyes down and eat a few. I let the conversation go on around me, about gardens and stuff I need never comment on. I try to stay calm. I can't blow it, there's too much at stake.

CHAPTER 24

'Right,' Ian says jovially, 'I think we may actually be able to eat now.'

He smiles and takes the burgers and chicken pieces off the barbecue. They smell good. My stomach rumbles but I'm not sure I'll be able to eat. I feel the sweat on my back and hate it. I don't want anyone to realise how uncomfortable I am. The food is handed around, and plates with napkins. There is a long table for everyone to sit at. It's laden with salads and fruit, bread, crackers and cheese. I watch as the LifeStar team congregate at one end. Justin and I sit at the other with Martha and Greta.

Martha turns to me. 'I'm so pleased you could come.' I gaze into her brown eyes and she smiles politely.

'Yes, well, thank you. And … you've got a beautiful home.' I don't know what to say.

'Do you like the art? Justin has no time for it, but I'm pleased if you can see something in it.'

'It's … I've never really thought of myself as someone who gets contemporary art, but here, in your home, it looks great.'

'Good. So a little later I'll introduce you to some of the pieces.' She gets up and glides back into the kitchen. Everything about them is smooth and slick, cultured and respectable. I'm completely out of place. I concentrate on trying to eat a chicken leg and salad. The sun beats down.

'Hey, come look at this,' Justin says drawing my attention to a book Joyce has opened before him. I go over and stand at the side of his chair, glad of the distraction.

Joyce seems pleased with the attention. 'This is my latest in the "Great and Gifted" series. Albert Einstein. I try to make complex subjects as accessible as possible for young readers.'

Justin looks at me briefly and I can see from his expression he's not convinced. 'You can't make E=MC squared easy. I mean it is to me, obviously,' he boasts. 'I get the maths but I appreciate most people don't.'

'I like to focus on personality,' Joyce explains, turning the pages. 'He was a great humanitarian. After the atom bomb was created, he said he wished he'd been a watchmaker, he was so appalled at the consequences.'

'He made a mistake,' Anton says easily. He turns to Joyce. I hadn't even realised he was listening. 'Creating the atom bomb was necessary. The world was at war and it brought the war to an end. Einstein's knowledge was crucial.'

'Anton, I hope you're not questioning my wife's admirable work.' Bill smiles facetiously.

'Far from it. I'm questioning Einstein's regret. Weapons of mass destruction are an unfortunate but necessary evil. They keep our enemies at bay. It's the principle of deterrence.'

I'm still, listening. I can't believe the direction the conversation has taken. 'Shouldn't science be used to better people's lives rather than destroy them?' I ask. What am I doing? I shouldn't be attracting attention to myself.

Bill looks at me and seems almost amused. 'In an ideal world, yes. If only we lived in an ideal world.'

Justin lets his hand drop to the side of his chair and then nudges my leg hard; I need to stop.

Bill continues. 'Scientists everywhere are working on many new and possible technologies. It's essential we're ahead of them and certainly not behind.' I think he likes the sound of his own voice. 'When guns were first developed, those peoples and nations without them were defeated, they were subjugated. What would have happened if Hitler had made the atom bomb first and not the Americans? We certainly wouldn't be living in the free democratic society we have today. So the realities of power never change and we all work within that.'

I know I daren't say any more and move to get a burger. I have to stretch over Chloe to reach them. I can smell her perfume and she crosses her legs, her skirt rising higher up her thigh. I take a seat away from them near Greta.

'Aren't they a bore?' she whispers to me under her breath. She glances at Martha and they exchange a conspiratorial smile. 'Why do some men like to talk about power so much?'

'They can't help it,' Martha says frankly.

Justin looks across at his mother and grins. 'No. We're charged with testosterone.'

'I think it's personality more than hormones, Justin,' Martha says indulgently. 'And, of course, the structures in our society which encourage it. I do sometimes wonder whether if women were in charge, and I mean really in charge, politically, if there wouldn't be a lot more talk of cooperation and a lot less of domination.'

Sasha smiles at Anton and places her hand on his knee. He smiles back.

'What do you think, Sasha?' Justin asks, his eyes fixed on her.

'I think Martha's right,' she says, relaxed.

'Anton, do you like a woman in charge?' he asks provocatively. I didn't think he'd try to wind up his father's colleagues.

'Sometimes, Justin,' Anton says with ease.

Justin smiles maliciously.

'Martha, you know fifty per cent of the office are women,' Ian says quickly, drawing attention away from Justin.

'The office, darling,' Martha says, 'but not the scientific team.'

'Aren't we missing the point?' Bill says condescendingly. 'All human beings – male or female – have a will to power. It's just a fact. I like what Brian used to say, "We've civilised the will to power into the pursuit of excellence." Surely that's something we can all agree on, the pursuit of excellence. After all, isn't that what art strives for as much as science?' He smiles pleasantly at Martha and Greta.

'Are you talking about Brian Minster?' Justin asks.

I look down. I can't meet his eye but I'm willing him to stop.

'Don't you sometimes wonder why the best scientist among you went and joined the Disciples?'

Oh, God, no. What is he doing?

'Justin,' Ian warns.

'He made a serious mistake,' Bill says slowly and calmly.

'What mistake was that?' Justin asks, goading.

'He believed in something, in someone, and belief never ends well.'

'Or maybe he didn't believe in anything?' Justin says. 'You can talk about power and excellence but there's also morality. "Each day we have a choice. A moral choice. Do we choose freedom over subjugation? Do we choose knowledge over ignorance? Do we allow ourselves to be downtrodden or do we understand we have collective power? And once we've made that choice – we fight for it."' He's just recited a quote from the Disciples.

I'm afraid to look up, to meet Ian's eye or to observe Chloe's expression. There is a long, tense silence.

Then Martha speaks in a cool, polite voice. 'Luke, shall I show you some Deleggianis?'

I turn to her. The tension defuses a little but I've no idea what she's on about.

'He's my favourite contemporary Italian artist,' she

137

explains. 'Not that he lives in Italy anymore, but Manhattan.'

I nod, yes. I don't care about her art but it will get me away from the table and out of the garden. Justin is unpredictable and I've no idea why Chloe is here. I follow Martha inside, glancing back. It's clear from their expressions that Justin and Ian are fuming with each other. I've only been here a short time, but the situation is completely out of control.

CHAPTER 25

I follow Martha to her study. It's a large spacious room with a wooden desk and a bookcase packed with oversized volumes on art.

'Have you read them all?' I ask, relieved we're alone.

'They're books you look through as much as read. But yes, I've read them all.'

We walk over to a stylish shelving unit with a variety of ornaments displayed upon it. Some of them look grotesque sculptures to me, but there are two beautiful objects made from glass.

'I love these,' I say, pointing to them. 'The colours are … they're amazing.'

'Yes, aren't they? You've spotted the Deleggianis for yourself. He tries to capture nature within the structure of the glass. In these two he's gone for birds, the kingfisher and the goldcrest, but he's done tigers, snow leopards other animals too. He's taken feathers, ground them down then diffused them through the glass. The impression is rather startling – flecks of colour and light. I love the translucent quality of the blue, orange and gold.'

'Do you mean he's used actual feathers?' I ask.

'Yes. But only from dead birds, he doesn't kill them. Apparently, people send them to him. Obviously, to find either a dead kingfisher or goldcrest is rare, but it is possible.'

Something about that reply sends a shiver down my spine. I might just hate her.

'I think feathers are powerful,' I say. 'I'm not sure they should be used in art.'

She looks at me for a long moment. 'Not many people think like you, but I would agree feathers are powerful. Although that's exactly why they make the art so beautiful.'

We hear footsteps behind us. 'Martha, I'm so sorry but as I said earlier I've got to go.' It's Sasha. 'It's been wonderful. Thank you for having me, but duty calls.'

'Must you go so soon?' Martha asks, although she's clearly been expecting this. 'But of course, I understand. Ageing relatives.' She shrugs sympathetically.

They lean into one another to kiss on the cheek, the kind of kiss where you don't actually touch the other person's face.

'I'm glad you've convinced Anton to be sensible about things,' she whispers into Sasha's ear. They release each other. 'I'll see you out.' Martha smiles and starts to walk down the hallway towards the front door. Sasha is about to follow then turns briefly to me. Her face alters, the polite smile gone. Her eyes spark with rage and anxiety. Her lips mouth silently, 'Get out, now!'

I freeze. It is Chloe, she's still a Disciple. She walks away, her pace slow and measured; she doesn't look back. My thoughts swim and collide into each other. My hands tremble and I'm glad for a few moments alone. Chloe is going out with Anton, one of Ian's team. I suddenly see it clearly. The Disciples are infiltrating LifeStar Corporation. I didn't think they could do such a thing, but then I never thought they could break into Colchester House. I almost whimper. I've not trusted Gil. I didn't believe what he said about avenging my father's death, but that's what they're in the process of doing. And Chloe's rage, I get it: I can seriously mess it up for them. She wants me out of here.

'Was Mum boring you to death?' Justin's found me. 'She must have been – I don't think I've seen you look so serious.'

I have to focus. He comes into the room and wraps his arm around my shoulder. 'Let's get you a drink.'

'I need to go,' I say suddenly. 'I'm sorry but I'm …' I can't think what to say. There's no ageing relative. I can't even mention my sister. For a second I think of inventing a football team, one I play with Sunday afternoons, but I'm not sure I can bluff it.

Justin shakes his head. 'Shut the fuck up,' he says gently with a smile. There is no backing out.

I follow him into the kitchen and then the garden. The sun is blasting down on the patio. Greta is half lying, half sitting in her chair, her eyes closed as she takes in the sun's rays. The atmosphere seems more relaxed.

'Sasha's lovely,' Martha says.

'Isn't she?' Anton smiles. 'To be honest, after Catherine, I'd given up hope … but life can surprise you.'

'And you said she's moving in?' Bill asks.

'Hopefully, that's the plan in the next few months … we're still deciding on the exact date. She's got to give notice on her lease.'

'It's all rather quick,' Joyce says.

Anton shrugs and smiles. 'Sometimes you just know it's right.'

I sit down and help myself to some grapes. Listening to them, I realise the Disciples have been working on this for a while. They could be close to getting what they want. I watch the juice of the black grapes bleed onto my fingers. An image from the dream flashes through my mind. I live with so much fear, but now …? Gil knows what he's doing. What if I leave this to him? I needn't take any more risks. There'll be no more lying to Charley and Flint. I won't have to take advantage of Justin. In truth, I know we can't better what the Disciples might do, especially as I can't see any way of leaking the information safely. I've not even started to discuss that with Justin. But now … I can leave it to the Disciples. What a relief.

'Want some cheese?' Justin offers as he cuts himself a large slice of brie.

'Yeah, I will thanks.' My appetite is returning. I have a way out. I'm not sure what I say to Justin except perhaps I'm bottling it, I can't go through. He'll think me a coward but that's alright. Chloe's face said it all: *Don't mess it up for us.*

Justin places a glass of white wine in front of me. 'It's chilled. You'll definitely want this with the cheese.'

I don't refuse it. I'm happy to sit and eat for a while; it delays dealing with Justin. Joyce is describing the route they took on a recent trip to China, what they saw and why they'd recommend it.

'I've always fancied Japan more than China,' Ian says. The conversation continues. The afternoon goes on. Eventually, Justin catches my eye. He indicates we should go inside. I realise I can't delay any longer.

We get up slowly and walk indoors.

'It's so hot out there,' he says.

'Yeah,' I agree.

He opens two cans of coke and passes me one. I pick it up but notice my hands are shaking slightly. That's strange.

'You're dehydrated,' he says, observing them.

It's the heaviest can I've held. I raise it and place it against my forehead, suddenly wanting the cold metal on my skin.

'Come upstairs,' he says softly, 'and I'll show you what I found.'

I hesitate. I lower the coke and gulp some down. 'Maybe … maybe not.'

'You're not backing out on me?' His eyes fill with panic. 'Please don't do that,' he says. He seems more vulnerable than aggressive.

'I … I feel a bit …' I glance around. I'm finding it hard to focus. 'I feel a bit … faint.' I'm giddy. I try to remember what I've eaten. Nothing unfamiliar. Yet I want to either run to the bathroom and vomit or sit down and put my head between my knees, maybe both.

'You've gone very pale,' Justin says.

I feel so ill. I watch the can of coke slip out of my hand and hit the floor. The liquid spills out. My legs start to crumple, I'm going down. The room fades around me. Darkness and silence.

CHAPTER 26

A voice through the dark. 'His breathing's too shallow.'

I struggle, I need air; my lungs are empty.

'Dominic, wake up.' A different voice. Louder.

My eyelids flutter, open. I'm staring at someone. Brown beard, moustache, seen him before. What's his name? A fragment of memory. Bill, that's it. He's holding something against my face.

'Just stay calm and breathe deeply. It's oxygen. Only oxygen.'

I feel the mask on my skin. He called me Dominic. How does he know I'm Dominic? I want to tell him I'm Luke but I can't speak.

Beyond his shoulder, they come into view: Justin and Ian. They're serious and silent. I want Justin to understand something is wrong, very wrong. He needs to get help, but I've no idea if he will.

I keep breathing, afraid, until breathing feels easier.

'Okay,' Bill says. 'You can put him under again.'

Everything fades away.

I wake. My eyes struggle to open, the lashes sticky. It takes a while to feel my body. I'm lying on a bed, resting on my right side and partially on my stomach. How did I get here? I try to focus. Desk in front of me, photos on the wall, a grainy shot of Gil Zimmerman. I'm in Justin's room.

There's a clock on the desk, a huge digital clock. Time: 10.37 a.m. The temperature: 22.4 degrees. The day and date. It's Tuesday. Tuesday … I don't understand. The last thing I remember is … Sunday.

'How are you feeling?' I turn to the doorway. It's Ian, dressed in a suit, ready to go to work.

My mouth is very dry. 'What happened?'

'You collapsed. Some sort of allergic reaction – we considered calling an ambulance but … well, I know how you feel about the authorities. We decided against it.' He speaks without emotion.

'Bill, I remember Bill. And struggling to breathe.'

'Yes, Bill trained as a doctor.'

I watch Ian. I've no idea what happened, but I understand he's lying.

'Where's Justin?' I ask, anxious.

'He's gone to see Martha's sister and his cousin. They're all in Switzerland for a few days.'

I realise I'm never going to see Justin again. He's been bundled off out of the way. Switzerland is a neutral country. Does that mean he's safe?

'You'll probably want a shower,' Ian offers. He motions to where he's left a towel on the desk chair. 'You should feel better after that.'

I notice my mobile's on Justin's desk. 'Did you try to phone anyone?' If they looked at my mobile they'll have seen Charley's and Flint's numbers; they'll know I'm still in contact with them.

'We considered it, but couldn't get past the security login. Is there somebody we should have called?'

Relief, they don't know about Charley and Flint.

'Is there someone you'd like me to contact now?' he asks.

'No. I … just need to get to work.' How will I explain this to Magda?

'The bathroom's just there.' He indicates. 'I'll be in my study.'

145

I watch him walk away. Nothing makes sense. I've never had an allergic reaction in my life, let alone one that knocked me out for two days. Everything around me looks normal. Justin's room. The hallway beyond it. Ian's house. Yet none of it is normal; it's a lie. I have to get out of here.

I try to sit up but I'm too groggy. I manage to crawl to the bathroom. I put on the shower and sit in the cubicle, the water thrashing down on me. It helps me feel inside my body again. I notice my arms and hands. There are specks of blood on each one, like the skin has been pierced. Did they use a needle on me? I stare at them. My blood. What if they've taken some of my blood? The warm water keeps flowing. I slowly understand. They've taken blood, they've got my DNA. It's the one thing my father said they must never get. Samples of my DNA.

My mind starts screaming but I have to stay silent. Get away. Hide. The danger I'm in is incalculable. Ian, Bill, LifeStar: they've got something I'd never give anyone. What will they do next?

I remember when I accused Ian of working for the police or MI5. 'Good God,' he'd said, 'you've got some imagination. They don't employ people like me.' I believed him, but who he is working for? I've misjudged everything.

I have to warn Charley and Flint. They must run. I don't know where we're going to hide but we'll find somewhere, we have to. My eyes sting. How could I have messed up so badly? At what point did Ian and his LifeStar team plan this? During lunch or days before? And Justin's gone; does he have any idea what they're involved in? What danger might he be in too, but then I remember Ian always protects him, one way or another. Justin's in Switzerland.

At last, I'm fully awake. I leave the bathroom, dry and dress quickly. Nothing matters now but getting away. I look beyond the bedroom door. The hallway is empty. Ian's study is out of sight. What's he doing there? I charge down the stairs. I don't stop to see where Ian is, I just fly towards the front door, open it and go.

Run, I scream at my legs. *Run!* And then I realise I don't know where I'm running to. I can't go home. I have to protect Charley. I switch on my phone, my hands shaking so violently I almost drop it. I ring her number. The line is dead. It doesn't even ring, there's nothing. The world spins and I lean against a wall. I can't faint. I almost smash the phone in terror and despair. But I refuse to believe she's gone, I won't accept that; they can't have got her. Or is that why I'm standing here, because they want me to take them to her?

I glance behind me. I can't see anyone but that doesn't mean they aren't chasing me. I duck into a side alley behind some shops. My fingers fumble dialling the number. I listen as the call rings out and then the automated voice at the other end, 'Please leave your message after the tone.'

'Gil.' I sound like I'm being strangled. 'Gil, I'm sorry, I got everything wrong. I'm in trouble. I'm in such fucking trouble and I need your help. And Charley and Flint. Please … please, help us.'

I can't continue. I'm crying. The magnitude of my mistake is hitting home. In trying to complete my father's work, I've done the one thing he warned me never to do. I lean over and retch, sick to the pit of my being, but no food comes up. I haven't eaten for days.

I realise I probably don't have much longer to live. They've got my DNA. They'll want to catch us and then experiment on us; Dad couldn't have made his warning clearer. And like my father, I'll die with everything left undone. Only one thing counts now. I head to the station. I buy a one-way ticket to Mary. I know I'll never come back.

CHAPTER 27

'Dominic, what are you doing here?' I stare at Gregory, his large round face and his tall stocky body. 'You look like you've been dragged through a hedge backwards.'

I need to speak but the words won't come.

'Jesus,' he mutters. He gazes round the shop, the rows of tinned food, canned drinks and baskets of fruit and veg. No customers are present. He steps out from behind the counter, flips the Open sign to Closed and indicates I go to the storeroom at the back. I hear him breathing heavily behind me. I could switch on the light, I know the storeroom well enough, but I don't. Instead, we stand in shadow opposite each other.

'You're meant to be in London,' he says carefully.

I nod, yes, and shake my head, no, at the same time.

I finally manage to speak. 'I'm in trouble. They're after me.'

'Oh, Jesus, Dominic.' He exhales. 'What have you done?'

My lower lip trembles. I look up at the ceiling. There's the long tube bulb that often flickers. I turn to Gregory again. 'LifeStar ... and MI5, I think maybe both of them. S'all the same really. And ... don't know where Charley and Flint are. Can't go home.'

'Dominic, you're in that much trouble and you choose to come here?' he says, bewildered.

I wince. It feels hard to breathe. 'I need to see Mary. I

don't know how much longer I've got to live and I want to say goodbye to her.'

'My daughter,' Gregory says, his voice trembling, 'who you say you love. You're in that much danger and you're bringing it to us. I thought you understood!'

I let out a sob. 'I'm sorry,' I whisper. 'I … I thought I could redeem something for my father only I messed up. I got it wrong. I never wanted this to happen. Everything's out of control.'

'Dominic, I've had to listen to you tell me a lot of lies over time, but right now,' he growls, 'I'm listening to too much of the truth. *You're* out of control.'

I want to disappear. All day I've wanted to disappear. I sat on the train coming here curled up pretending to sleep.

Gregory grows calmer, still. His voice drops to a whisper. 'Do our "friends" know?'

The tension in me lessens a fraction.

'I've a number for them. I left a message on an answer machine. I've no idea if or when they'll get it. And, they don't know I'm here – just that I'm in trouble.'

He listens, quiet. 'This is what you're going to do,' he says slowly. 'In a few minutes, you're going to go out of the back door and get into the pickup truck. I'm going to come out and drive you some distance from here. I'll leave you at a loch with some provisions, and then you're going to start praying.'

I swallow. 'Praying?'

'Praying that if I'm able to contact our friends they're going to be able to help you. And if not …' He shakes his head, upset.

I nod, although I'm not sure why. 'I had thought,' I say, 'on the way up, that one way out of this would be to ask you to shoot me. I know you've got a shotgun. For grouse or whatever.'

'Don't flatter yourself,' he says sharply. 'It would be a waste of shot.'

He drives while I lie flat in the back of the truck, a tarpaulin thrown over me. I feel both sick and relieved. Gregory's right to be mad at me, I'm putting them in danger, but I have to see Mary. Or is that also why I'm here, because I'm in danger and need to see him? Gregory can contact the Disciples and they're my only hope. I've totally fucked up and my stomach clenches in anguish.

The ride is uncomfortable; the truck bounces on the uneven road. I wonder where he's taking me, if it's to the loch we've all sat at together. I have such good memories from there but now … I might die in that place.

The truck stops. Gregory gets out and then yanks the tarpaulin off me. I gaze around. I do recognise it. I jump down.

'Here,' he says, and passes me a sleeping bag and a canvas backpack. 'Some food, matches, a torch.'

I nod, grateful.

'No point putting up a tent, it's summer. You'll find it cold but it won't kill you. And a tent's more visible.'

He moves to get back in the truck.

'Gregory,' I say, hoping he might wait a moment longer. 'Thank you.'

He pauses before hoisting himself back into the driver's seat. 'I don't know, Dominic, if helping you like this … I might be making the biggest mistake of my life.'

'No.' I shake my head. 'You're a good man, one of the best I've known. Thank you. Thank you for everything.'

He doesn't answer immediately. 'Get yourself out of trouble, Dominic. Please. For everyone's sake.'

He sits in the driver's seat and shuts the door. I let him drive off without saying another word. I didn't tell him I love him. I hope he knows I do.

CHAPTER 28

I am alone. I shiver, scanning the landscape. The loch, the grass that's grown high, and the hills beyond. I can see for miles. There's not another person about. And it will be light for hours yet. Usually, I like the fact it doesn't get dark until very late here, not in the summer. Yet now I'm running for my life, I want darkness to descend.

I look around for a quiet corner to hide in. But there are no corners and the whole place is quiet. I walk closer to the water's edge, unfold the sleeping bag and lie down. I'm exhausted, but sleep is a luxury I can't afford. I look up at the sky and wonder how they'll come for me. Will a helicopter suddenly come into view? Will a car screech across the landscape? Or maybe it won't happen at all? I'm actually safe. No one's following me. The Highlands are truly at the end of the world. I wonder if Dad felt safe before they shot him or if he knew he was going to die. I close my eyes a moment remembering the feel of his ashes between my fingers.

I nod off despite myself and when I wake the sun is sinking lower in the sky. There's something moving in the distance, a vehicle approaching. I gradually make out the outline of Gregory's pickup truck. It comes to a halt.

'Dominic.' It's Mary's distinctive voice.

I stand up and wave. She rushes towards me, her eyes full of anxiety. We embrace but she's speaking quickly.

'Dad said I shouldn't come, but he also knew I would.

He said he didn't know what you'd done but you'd gone too far.' Her words are running into each other, and I have to release our embrace for her to read my lips.

'Mary, I'm in trouble, serious trouble,' I start, aware I need to say it all and it will be blunt. 'I messed up and there are things I have to tell you and I don't have a lot of time.' I swallow, then say more slowly. 'I know you love me, Mary, and that matters more to me than anything. And I've told you many things, but there are some truths I've never shared with you. Not what I did with the Disciples, and not a secret … about my body.'

She looks at me and I see her struggling to understand. I continue, enunciating my words as clearly as I can. 'My father did something to me. To me and Charley, to our genes, to our DNA. And now there are people out there who want me. They want to understand what he did to us and how they can use it.'

She stands there, familiar and beautiful, yet bewildered. 'I don't understand, Dom.'

'There are qualities I have …' I drop my voice to a whisper although there's nobody else to hear. 'I can breathe underwater.'

'What?'

'I can breathe underwater and … maybe there's more, things that not even I know about or understand, but I fear somebody else does. LifeStar Corporation and possibly MI5. In the end, they get to know everything. They're going to come and get me, and I've no way of stopping them.'

'But Dominic, you're my boyfriend. You're just a regular guy.'

'Mary, I wish I was.'

She's silent. Her eyes dart here and there then rest on me.

'No … I don't want you to get hurt,' she whispers.

'Me neither,' I say, trying to hold my voice steady. 'But I probably will. So I want you to know, Mary, you're the best thing that's ever happened to me, and I love you. And whatever they do to me, that love is something they can never take away. I love you.'

There is more I have to say, but it's the hardest part. 'You need to find somebody else now. Somebody who can love you without causing you trouble and pain. I'm not a safe person for you to be with.'

'No, Dom.' She shakes her head.

'It's over, Mary,' I say slowly. 'We have no future. You must leave me, now.'

'No, Dom. I don't accept what you're saying. I don't accept any of it.'

I look around. It's getting dark. She's got to go, I can't protect her.

'I don't accept what you're saying.' Her eyes glisten.

'Mary, please. Go. I'm in danger and you must protect yourself. I've made a mistake, I got something really wrong. I thought I could make good my father's life, but I ignored all the danger signs and all the advice I was given. And there's no way I'm going to let you take the consequences of that with me.'

But she doesn't move. She just shakes her head.

'Please, Mary. Leave now. I beg you.'

Her eyes are wide and then her face is strangely serene. She almost smiles. 'I can protect you,' she says.

I shake my head. 'No, Mary. You're the sweetest, kindest person I know, but you cannot protect me. I'm not sure anybody can.'

'I can,' she says calmly, determined. 'Remember, I know the colour of your soul.'

There's nothing I can say to that; she loves me.

'I've got something with me.' She turns and heads back to the pickup truck. I think she's got Gregory's gun; it's more likely to get us killed than save us. She takes something out of the back. I'm unsure what it is, but it's wrapped in a blanket.

'Sit down,' she says.

I have no idea what's going on but the quickest way to get her out of here is to do as she says. Whatever she's got in mind, I sense I can't stop her. Then she walks back to the truck and returns with a bundle of twigs and a few logs. She starts to make a fire.

'Mary, this is crazy, we can't attract attention to ourselves like this.'

'It won't be for long, but it's important.'

She's good at kindling the twigs and wood, and it isn't long before there's a fire blazing hot and fierce. I'm just praying that no one can see it and they won't come until she's gone.

'Take off your top,' she says.

I unzip my jacket and put it on the ground.

'No, everything you've got on. Your chest needs to be bare.'

I hesitate a moment, but her expression tells me not to argue. The night air is cool and goosebumps rise on my skin.

'Lie back on the ground.'

Again, I hesitate. Yet her eyes are full of their own fire. I lie down. The ground is damp and cold. She folds back the blanket she is carrying and I see what's inside. It's the eagle wing from her room. She holds it in both hands and raises it above the flames.

And then I can't move. The ground has sucked me into its surface. Mary is standing by the fire and there are words, sounds, coming from her mouth. I think she's praying, praising, doing something I can't interpret. And I have no control; I can't fight the ground holding me or Mary's incantations. The beat of my heart grows louder, deeper, thumping. The blood in my veins feels hot and I'm afraid, really terrified, that I too will become fire. Mary turns to me, her face quite altered, wild and ecstatic. She walks towards me and puts the eagle's wing on my chest over where my heart is. I'm gasping for air and grasping at the ground. I'm losing myself. Mary pushes down on the feathers, pushing down on my heart.

'You are protected.' Her face is illumined by the fire. 'You are fearless and free.' She is like the priestess of a religion I do not know. 'And you will find your way back to me.'

I feel the heat of the wing scorching my skin and she presses it down harder and harder. I'm going to die – the beat of my heart is so powerful it can't be contained in my chest. I scream, my voice like an animal's in the night. Then it's over. Mary is breathing hard, her hands and a few feathers on my chest. The wing has gone. There is a layer of sweat on my body. I'm breathing fast, but Mary's eyes are calm.

I don't know what just happened. I won't try to explain it. But I can move again. I raise my hand to Mary's face and touch it, slowly, running my fingers across her cheeks, her lips. Then I hold her hair and bring her face down to mine. We kiss. The sex we have is urgent and intense. For some time afterwards, our bodies feel fused together. I can't speak and she stays silent. It is completely dark now. I have no idea how this night will end.

CHAPTER 29

I hold Mary as she sleeps, a strange, fidgety slumber. The fire's gone out but the air smells of burnt wood. Soon we will be separated, and I will never be able to explain what happened here tonight with her. I touch my chest; there's the soft smudge of ash on my skin. There is nothing else, no feather or bird bone, just my skin and ash.

I stare through the darkness and feel calm; I know it can't last. Gradually, a small light becomes visible in the distance. I hear the distant rumble of a motorbike. It comes closer. I prop myself up on my elbow, watching. There is no helicopter whirring above, no line of cars advancing, only a single bike. The rider is a silhouette in black leather and a helmet. I almost cry; I recognise him.

The bike comes to a halt. He removes his helmet. I can tell he's been riding a while, his hair's matted to his head with sweat. I can't see his eyes properly, not through the glare of the bike's light. He switches it off, and then I can't see his eyes because of the dark.

I try to speak but it takes a while. 'You've no idea how glad I am to see you.'

'I think I do,' Gil says.

'I messed up. I …' I hesitate. 'Charley and Flint, they need help too. You've got to find them.'

He stands still, but even in the dark I sense the power in his body, his presence.

'You disobeyed me,' he says coolly.

I swallow hard. 'Yes, I'm sorry.'

'Sorry may not be enough.'

'I know you'll punish me,' I say, wavering, 'but please, Charley and Flint. Don't punish them. They need your help.'

'Charley and Flint are safe.'

That stops me. 'They're with you?'

He nods. I wipe a tear from my cheek, relieved. 'Thank God. Thank you.'

Mary stirs beside me and on seeing Gil she sits up quickly.

'Go,' he says, and motions to the pickup truck.

Mary hesitates and Gil comes closer. He kneels down, facing her. 'Your father knows what he and you have got to do.' He's letting her read his lips. 'They will come for you and question you, but stay brave and you'll be alright. Your father will instruct you.'

Mary says nothing, but nods. We have been so close tonight but now she rises without turning to me. I watch her walk to the truck. She gets inside without meeting my eyes; I understand, she doesn't want to show emotion, not in front of Gil. She starts the vehicle and then drives off. Gil and I watch its lights diminish in the distance.

'I've wanted to keep her safe,' I whisper, taking in what Gil's said, 'I—'

'Before you say anything else, Dominic, we don't have a lot of time.' He turns to me. 'Empty your pockets.'

I pull out the side pockets on my trousers, they're empty. I reach for my jacket and retrieve my phone. He throws it on the ground and stamps on it. I clench my teeth but say nothing as I watch it disintegrate, the mechanism splintering apart. He turns to me.

'Anything else?'

I shake my head.

'Except they've probably embedded a tracking device in your body. It won't be far below the surface of your skin, but it's got to come out.'

I'm stunned, silent. And then I start to feel sick.

'You haven't felt it or seen it?' he asks.

I shake my head again.

'Then it's probably in your back.' He indicates I turn around. My torso is still naked and he runs his hands carefully down my spine. I shiver. Then he feels round my shoulders. I cry out as he touches the bullet wound. His fingers stay there.

'Those bastards.' He breathes deeply. He's found it.

'How are you going to get it out?' I ask, afraid. Nothing could have prepared me for this.

'With a knife,' he says softly.

'Oh, shit.' My legs wobble.

'Lie down on your stomach.'

My knees give way and then I'm flat on the ground. The softness of his voice is what scares me most. He sits on my back and his left knee pins my shoulder down.

'I can't breathe.' The pressure of his body on mine is intense.

'You don't need to.' And then he does it. I don't see the knife, it must have been in his pocket, but I feel it. The pain is excruciating; the wound is torn open and my mind fills with blinding white light. I can't breathe. I want to pass out. I scream but the sound is gurgled as I'm squashed beneath him. The world judders and then it's over. His grip lessens and I'm gasping. He lowers his right hand level with my eyes. His fingers are covered in blood, but it's there, a small metal object. He throws it towards the loch and we hear the plop as it hits the water. I imagine it sinking down.

'Stay still,' he says softly, 'while I apply some gauze to stem the bleeding.'

He walks to his bike, opens one of the panniers and removes a small box. I hear the sound of a spray and where I'd felt pain and blood it's suddenly very cold. His hand presses down on me, gentler this time. Then he straps the bandage in place. He puts the small box back and walks over to help me up. I stand but the world starts spinning.

'Don't faint,' he says, supporting the back of my neck. 'Just breathe deeply.'

I gulp down the night air. After a few moments he gets on the bike. I put on my clothes. He passes me a helmet and then I clamber on behind him.

'We'll be riding for a while,' he says. 'Whatever happens, don't let yourself fall asleep. You have to keep a grip. Okay?'

I think of the other time I got on a bike with him, the night of my seventeenth birthday. It was an old vintage model, nothing like this new one. He rode it like a maniac. But now I don't care how he rides, just that we get away. I put my arms around him and hold on tight.

'I won't fall asleep,' I promise.

CHAPTER 30

Gil brings the bike to a halt. We've been riding for hours. My body is stiff and cold, and he has to unfurl my fingers gripping him. We're outside a small country cottage. Through the dawn light I see fields around us; there isn't another building in sight. I feel numb, my thoughts suspended … no point trying to contemplate what happens next.

We enter the cottage. Gil doesn't turn on a light but guides me quickly to a side room. There is a camp bed and a few blankets. The place is cold and uninviting.

'You've got a few hours to get some kip,' he says, 'and then we'll talk.'

He leaves the room and I crash out exhausted.

Later, I'm shaken roughly. 'Wake up, Dominic.'

I open my eyes and I'm staring at Tom, Gil's second in command. I wasn't expecting to see him. His blond beard is longer than I remember, but his blue eyes are as hard as ever. Our relationship was difficult in the past but I don't doubt his authority. His presence is a sign of the trouble I'm in. I feel too tired to move but daren't say it.

'Charley and Flint are here now,' he says.

I sit up quickly. 'Okay.' I'm relieved. 'Thank you.'

He puts out his hand to help me up. He smiles, although it's not friendly. 'We might still shoot you yet,' he whispers.

He never liked me, and I know whatever follows isn't going to be easy. He takes me into a sparse kitchen. Charley and Flint are sitting at a large wooden table. Then my eyes fall on Baz, a Disciple we knew in the Highlands. I almost feel relief seeing his dark skin and short dreadlocks; his expression is serious but his eyes are kind. We all got on with Baz, Flint in particular. For a moment I wonder if that's why he's here. There's no sign of Gil.

Charley and Flint turn to me, their faces etched with anxiety and exhaustion. I want to hug my sister but she shakes her head.

'*I'm sorry*,' I whisper, silent. I'm choked. I've hurt them.

'What have you done, Dom?' Flint asks, bewildered.

Charley's eyes hold mine. 'You should have told us, Dom. How could you not have told us?'

Flint looks at the table and it's then I see my notebook, the one with the eagle feathers in it. I also hid Justin's letter inside.

'We got back from the park,' he says, his voice shaking slightly, 'and then Baz is at the door. I can't tell you what went through my mind. And we're trying to figure out what the hell you've been doing 'cause you're at the Pendletons', in serious fucking trouble, and we're going through your stuff trying to find some clue …' He's close to tears. He pulls Justin's letter out. I wonder how many times they've read it.

'I asked you, Dom, to tell me what was going on,' Charley says. 'I knew you were up to something. Didn't *I* have a right to know too?'

My throat is so tight I feel I'm being strangled. 'I'm sorry.' Never have two words felt so inadequate. 'I thought … I was trying to do it for Dad.'

'Sit down,' Tom says.

I walk behind Flint and Charley to the seat available for me. I'm stricken at how much I've hurt them. I kept secrets, I lied.

'You look like shit, Dominic,' Baz says. 'When did you last eat or drink?'

'I …' I shrug, 'days ago, I think.'

Tom opens a cupboard behind him; there are a few items inside. He passes me an energy drink and an energy bar. He gives them to Charley and Flint too. 'This is the best we can do.'

Flint rips the wrapping on his bar and eats it quickly, but I notice his hand is shaking.

'Dominic, you've got to eat something.' Tom watches me.

'I'm not hungry,' I say, aware of just how sick I feel.

'Drink first,' Tom says, 'then eat slowly.' Still, I don't move. 'That's a command.'

The tension between Charley, Flint and I is the worst I've known. It feels like a private situation we need to sort out, but Tom and Baz are here, and there's nothing private about what I've done.

I unscrew the bottled drink and take a few sips.

'*Please don't hate me,*' I whisper into Charley's head.

I start to eat the energy bar and know I have to keep it down.

Eventually, Gil enters the room. He looks groggy and walks over to the deep ceramic sink. He runs the cold tap and splashes water on his face. He stays there a few moments, wipes the water away then turns to us.

'We don't have a lot of time,' he says, his voice surprisingly strong. 'And you all need to understand what's happening.'

He stands tall while Tom and Baz remain sitting. 'You disobeyed me, Dominic. I commanded you to live a small, ordinary life. You didn't. I told you we'd avenge your father's death, and God knows why but you thought you could do better. You fuck up!'

His eyes burn into me and my skin itches. 'And now you're a significant problem we've got to deal with.'

There's a laptop on the table. Tom leans over, opens it and turns the screen to us.

'From the moment we finished interviewing your father,' Gil says, 'we've been working on infiltrating LifeStar Corporation, getting somebody close enough to Dr Pendleton's team to be able to access the information your father couldn't get to us. All we needed was time to complete a highly sensitive operation.'

His eyes fix on me again. Tom brings up an image of Anton and Chloe smiling at the camera.

'You met *Sasha*, Dominic. And you almost blew her cover. Do you imagine what Chloe's doing is easy? Or have any idea of the price she could pay for her actions? Anton keeps his secrets and he also talks too freely. And every piece of information she gets she has to judge how to handle. We've had to work very hard trying to understand what's been going on with you. And I'm afraid you've all been in trouble for some time,' Gil says pointedly. 'We only understood just how much when Chloe made contact on Saturday night to tell us Sunday lunch was a set-up.'

His gaze moves to Charley and Flint. 'I repeat, you've *all* been in trouble for some time, although Dominic has excelled himself.' His voice is caustic. 'I'll start at the beginning.'

Our eyes meet. I brace myself for what he'll say next.

CHAPTER 31

Tom moves the laptop closer to us. He brings up a series of photos of Ian Pendleton.

Gil speaks in a calmer voice. 'Dr Ian Pendleton, Research Manager and Advisor, knew your father was a brilliant scientist, but he also considered him a maverick. Maverick enough to have possibly interfered with the genes of his own children. Those were private thoughts, conjecture, and they would have remained that if he hadn't recognised you, Dominic, in Coffee Primo. When he first approached you, he was acting alone. He had nothing to do with the police or MI5.' Gil pauses briefly as Tom brings up a picture of Pendleton's home. 'The items he gave you from your father's office were genuine. But he's an ambitious man. And when you sat in his house having a drink, touching his furniture, taking a piss, you left traces of your DNA – just as he wanted.'

My stomach turns. I remember it all; I had no idea.

'The mistake *he* then made was not anticipating what would happen once he ran your data through LifeStar's system. It was flagged up: it wasn't normal. Something exceptional was revealed. And that's when things got difficult for him and his team. MI5 got involved. Ian, Bill Grange, Anton Levinsky, Fiona Crane, they were all put under pressure and then so were you.'

I turn to my cousin and my sister but their attention is focused on Gil.

He continues. 'Charley and Flint told me about the break-in at your flat. I don't believe it was a criminal act, however much they made it look like one. It was MI5. They'll have been looking for evidence and planting a bug or two. They've probably been listening to your conversations for weeks.'

There's a stunned hush. Flint pales. Charley's breathing hard.

'We … we couldn't have known,' I say.

'No,' Gil acknowledges. 'And we didn't know either, but I can guarantee you, from what Charley and Flint have told us, that's what happened.'

I think of that night. 'We spoke about the gun, the one you'd given me. Charley had got rid of it but still we spoke about it. I think I mentioned the Disciples.'

Gil nods. 'The question you may ask yourselves, then, is why, given they had all this information about you, including your DNA, did they not arrest you?'

'Why didn't they?' Flint asks because it doesn't make sense. 'They were looking for us before. Brian always warned us against being caught and they found us.'

'Because they made a strategic decision,' Gil says carefully. 'From their point of view, they could arrest you whenever they wanted. They knew exactly where you were. And the jobs you were doing and the way you were living meant you weren't an immediate threat to security. The Disciples, however, *are*. They've been finding it very difficult to get us, so … Dominic provided them with an opportunity.'

Tom brings up another picture on the laptop. It's Justin, only he's wearing a suit and he looks a lot older.

'Enter Justin Pendleton. Ian does have a stepson. He's studying History of Art and is currently spending a year in Japan. The man you know as Justin Pendleton is Agent Greene, one of MI5's most talented young recruits.'

The room spins, I fear I might faint.

'How did you describe him to Charley, Dominic? As difficult and unpredictable, messed up by his own father's death and wanting to join the Disciples?' Gil watches me. 'They will have worked hard on that story and they played you well.'

Tom's eyes fix on mine. 'Without raising a finger against you, without any formal interrogation, they got all the information they wanted from you.'

'Stop.' I can't bear it.

Tom shakes his head like I should have known better. 'And no doubt he never stopped telling you how much he wanted to join the Disciples. If only you could help him.'

'I never let on,' I retort. 'I always insisted I had nothing to do with you.'

'I believe you,' Gil says. 'When did Justin give you the letter?'

'It was not long after the break-in. He just walked into Coffee Primo and gave me it.'

'It's good, Dominic. We think a lot of what's in it is accurate. They hoped you would pass that letter on to us, and because we'd interviewed your father they knew anything too fake would ring our alarm bells *if* you'd passed it on to us. However … what we don't know, Dominic, is what happened next. You received that letter, you didn't give it to us, but not long after Justin learnt what your father confessed to you about LifeStar, and of your desire to expose that truth. And, as if that wasn't bad enough, he also saw you had a bullet wound on your left shoulder, which they took as evidence of your *operational* involvement with us. What happened, Dominic, that he got such vital information from you?'

I look down, my cheeks hot. I try to answer, but it would be easier if the ground swallowed me up. 'They … Justin took me. We went … wild swimming. I thought we were becoming friends. It never crossed my mind, I mean, I could never have known it was a set-up.'

'Wild swimming?' Tom says slowly.

I nod, but this is excruciating. 'Justin … he drove us out of London. We were just meant to talk about the letter. I'd hoped I could get him to find some other documents. But then we got to this lake, this stream, and I hadn't initially wanted to do it, it was all his idea, but he just stripped off and dived in. He seemed so natural and uninhibited like you might be, and in the end I followed him.'

'Shit, Dom,' Flint says turning to me. 'You met the guy and didn't tell us.'

'I'm sorry,' I mutter.

'Natural and uninhibited like we might be,' Tom repeats. 'Would you strip off to go wild swimming, Gil?'

'I probably would.'

'Yeah, I probably would too,' Tom says.

I close my eyes, humiliated.

'Didn't he play you well, Dominic?' Gil says softly. 'He knew every button to press.' He's still, thinking. 'So after that episode, it's clear they felt they had enough evidence to play their endgame. They invited you to Sunday lunch. They drugged you and you woke up two days later. They took a range of body samples, getting what they wanted, and they managed to scare the shit out of you so badly you had no alternative but to finally … *finally* come to us. And if Chloe hadn't worked so quickly they'd have picked up Charley and Flint too, leaving you utterly stranded. We were lucky to get to them in time.'

Flint, Charley and I don't move or speak, trying to process all he's told us.

Gil turns to Tom and Baz. 'They implanted the tracking device by the bullet wound.'

'Painful,' Baz says.

'And expensive, I've not seen one like that before. They're getting more sophisticated.' Gil turns back to us. 'To help you understand the gravity of the situation, and just how much you need us, I'm going to play you part of the inter-view we recorded with your father.'

Tom activates it on the laptop.

Gil's voice comes out of the speaker. 'And Dominic and Charley ... they can breathe underwater. What ... what was your thinking when you did that?'

There is a pause on the recording. I feel light-headed. Charley glances across at me, anxious.

We hear my father's voice. 'At the time ... I was thinking about lung capacity in terms of oxygenating the blood, en-suring oxygen got to their brains, the heart, limbs. It could enhance their performance and, in a polluted world, they could still breathe easily. It all sounds ...' Quiet. A period of silence. 'The truth now though,' Dad says, determined, 'is if they succeed in actualising Olethros, if they ever use that weapon, the only chance of survival will be to submerge yourself in water. Completely. Fully. Probably for three to four hours. The toxic agent can't survive beyond that, and it can't penetrate water.'

Again, a pause on the recording. Then Gil's voice. 'Are you saying that Dominic and Charley, in essence, have within their genetic make-up the capacity to survive that weapon?'

My father replies, 'Yes, that's what I'm saying. And maybe even ... they won't complete its production without that knowledge. Part of LifeStar's remit was to consider an antidote as well as the weapon. That's how Ian, Bill, all of them are able to live with themselves. They'll go home at night and pretend what they're doing is acceptable. '

Tom stops the recording. My father's voice was clear: the simplicity of what he said, and the terror of it. I'm shaking. Charley is too. Flint looks sick.

'Now you understand why I told you to live a small, ordinary life,' Gil says slowly. 'But you didn't. You need to disappear. All of you. Quickly.'

CHAPTER 32

The room is silent. We are too shocked to speak. Suddenly, a phone bleeps. It's Tom's. He reads the message quickly.

'Something's wrong,' he says, urgent. 'Spike's reporting there's too much activity in the village. Too many cars passing through.'

Another moment of silence. I watch their faces tense. In the distance is a mechanised sound, but I can't make it out. All three Disciples withdraw a pistol from their clothing. Seconds pass and the sound gets louder, clearer. It's the rotating blades of a helicopter. Gil looks up and I watch as fear masks his face. I didn't think it was possible, but he's afraid.

'We're in trouble,' he says, his eyes alert.

'Who's betrayed us?' Baz hisses. His hand tightens round his pistol. 'We made this watertight.'

Tom's eyes focus on me. 'Dominic.'

I feel the blood drain from my limbs. 'What?'

'We searched Charley and Flint fully, frisked their clothes and checked over everything. So you …' His expression hardens. 'You, Dominic, are the only person who could have brought them here. Whatever you've got on you … or in you.'

Gil and Baz's eyes fix on me. I let my hand slip to the only thing I've got for security, my father's pen, like a talisman because everything is out of control. The pen I took from our flat … the flat MI5 infiltrated. I withdraw it slowly from my trousers and place it on the table. How could I not have remembered it when Gil asked me to empty my pockets?

'Oh God, no.' Charley whispers, distraught.

My hands are trembling. 'My father's pen,' I say, hoarse.

A terrible silence follows then Tom leans over to take the pen. He pulls off the lid and unscrews the body. Something small and metallic sits within it; it's not an ink cartridge or font. 'What the fuck?' He smashes it down on the table but even then it doesn't break.

'Dominic, what have you done?' Gil's eyes are dark pools, his voice low.

I think it's possible we're going to die. The seconds splinter as dread invades my body. The helicopter draws closer, the sound of its rotating blades intensifying.

Gil barks. 'Baz, you take Flint. And Tom, Charley. Lose yourselves. Disappear.'

Baz and Tom rise quickly, but Charley and Flint hesitate. I turn to my sister and cousin. Our eyes meet. I sense this is the end; I want them to forgive me. I want them to know I love them. I pray they can see it in my eyes because I can't speak.

I turn back to Gil. His face twitches with tension. 'Go!' he shouts at Tom and Baz. They drag Charley and Flint from their chairs. Gil focuses on me.

'Leave him,' Tom instructs. 'You know they won't kill him. They've always wanted them alive.'

Everything is disintegrating.

'If you take him, Gil,' Tom warns, 'you'll die.'

The room swims before me. Gil's expression is hard; his eyes feel like they're burning through me.

'Leave him!' Tom shouts. 'We don't have time. There are other things we can do. We'll take out the Kendrick facility, but you can't take Dominic.'

'No,' Charley shrieks.

'Shut up.' Tom points his pistol at her. 'We could kill you both, that's another option.'

Gil's eyes are locked on mine. Every fibre in my body is willing him to take me with him. His hand tightens on his gun. I close my eyes. We know each other well enough; if he's going to leave me, he's got to shoot me because I won't be taken alive by MI5.

'Let's go!' Baz orders. I hear the door open and feel a rush of air from outside.

'Don't leave him,' Charley wails.

'Go! All of you!' It's Gil.

'Leave him, Gil,' Tom strains. 'He'll kill you.'

Gil is breathing hard. 'No,' he says. 'They'll have to catch me first, and they're not going to do that.'

I open my eyes.

'Dominic, you come with me.'

We charge out of the cottage to the three motorbikes waiting outside. It only takes seconds for us to mount them, helmets on and then we're heading away from each other. I don't say goodbye to Charley and Flint, there isn't time. I just grip Gil's jacket, aware every second is crucial. The helicopter is circling above us; it seems to follow, but then it holds back. It disappears. The road and the sky above grow quiet. We are racing through countryside. The tension in me releases a fraction. For a moment I even imagine we're safe.

But we're not safe. I hear sirens although I can't locate where they're coming from; the police are behind us or chasing us on some parallel road. Yet it's the helicopter's reappearance that chills me to the bone. I glance momentarily behind. It has two huge rotors and there's a camera filming everything. It's the kind of helicopter I've seen in films, where they can pull back the door and a marksman can take aim. I cling to Gil. They'll come closer to shoot. This is what they've wanted – they've been waiting for this moment. I'll feel a bullet. My mind anticipates the worst. We'll be brought down. The bike will crash to the ground and our bodies will go flying. We'll be smashed, strewn apart. Death will be agony.

We keep moving. No shots are fired. 'You know they won't kill him,' Tom had said. Is that why we're still alive? They can't target Gil when our bodies are so close together. What an insane, mad triumph. I never thought I'd be happy to be a human shield, but I am. Charley will be protecting Tom too.

Time slows and then I have no sense of time. Gil stays focused on the route ahead; we swing round corners, flash past cars, and stay off the main road. We seek high hedges, trees, back roads and fields. I think he knows where we're going, but even if he doesn't I trust him anyway.

The sirens fade and amplify, the helicopter is unrelenting, and the bike's fuel gauge runs low. If we don't refuel soon we'll just stop. Gil takes us past fields and then we're on a wide tarmac road. The traffic increases and we reach a roundabout. Turning left, the bike judders. I can't believe it will end like this. But there's a petrol station ahead. We pull in and stop at a free pump. Gil turns off the engine, gets off the bike and unscrews the fuel cap.

'Shit,' he says dropping it, his fingers fumbling. He slams the petrol nozzle into the bike and lets the fuel flow. Every second feels interminable; they'll only be getting closer. He pulls the nozzle out of the bike, screws the cap back on and starts the engine. The attendant runs from his kiosk shouting at us. Gil aims his pistol. Oh, fuck, no. The bullet explodes on the concrete near the man's feet. I hear a scream but we're out of there. I hold Gil tight. We've got fuel, it took time, but they haven't caught up.

We head off the main road again. The bike and our clothes are filthy with dust and dirt. My throat is parched, my eyes too dry. The sirens continue. The helicopter disappears, but not for long. I fear they may never stop.

Then, we reach an area of thick, dense woodland. Gil slows the bike as we head into the trees. He brings us to a halt, gets off and opens the pannier. He grabs a bottle of water and removing his helmet pours it over his head. He gulps some down then passes it to me, but his hand's shaking. I watch him retrieve his phone and gaze at it. He looks exhausted, haggard.

'Tom and Baz have lost them,' he says, hoarse. 'You … you need to understand what's happening now.' The tone of his voice makes me shiver. 'They're not going to stop until they've got me.'

I listen but can't hear. 'No,' I say. I understand only that Charley and Flint are safe. That means we can be too.

'I will be dead by the end of the day,' he says starkly. 'They've let the others go because they can afford to. They've got me and they've got you.'

I'm silent. Gil doesn't say things like this.

'Tom was correct – they want you alive. You're too valuable to kill. Everything they've done, in its way, has been to protect you while ensnaring me.'

'Gil, no, stop.' I'm afraid now. He's got to shut up.

'As soon as they have a clear shot – they'll bring me down.'

'No,' I say. 'No! That's not what's going to happen.' I shake my head. 'I won't let them have a clear shot. I'll cling to you like a limpet – they won't get you.'

Gil says softly, 'I'm sorry I failed to protect your father, and I'm sorry, Dominic, I've failed to protect you.'

'No!' I insist.

'I'm heading for the coast now. I'll die in my own way. Over the cliffs and into the sea.' He doesn't shout, he's almost whispering. He's talking about his death. I refuse to hear it.

'I'm coming with you.' He must know I won't leave him.

Our eyes meet; his are full of sadness. 'Only to the cliff edge. Then we part ways.'

'No.'

'You will surrender, Dominic,' he says calmly. 'I won't tell you they'll be kind to you. They won't. But you'll find you can bargain with them. You'll be able to have a life.'

I listen and feel the tears on my cheeks. I finally realise what this means. I have failed, my father failed, and now … Gil too.

'Gil, no. We keep running. You can't die, I won't surrender.' Yet even as I say it I know that's not true.

He looks at me for a quiet moment. 'I never imagined I'd grow old, Dominic,' he says without fear. 'But … I will give them something to remember.'

There is nothing else I can say. We hear the helicopter circling above, the sirens growing louder, and then we get back on the bike and race out into the open again.

CHAPTER 33

I grip Gil but my mind starts to numb. Every option I face is unbearable. Gil dying. Me surrendering. Both of us dying. Charley and Flint living the rest of their lives without me. Mary and Gregory, I love them both, but I've only brought them trouble. And Gil … I cannot imagine the world without him, his wild, defiant spirit. The Disciples will lose their leader, but Gil *is* the Disciples. And Gemma, I see her crying. And somewhere his son, a child who will grow up without a father. It's unbearable, yet I can't prevent it.

It starts to rain. The oppressive heat that has gone on for days breaks. Lightning flashes across the sky. Thunder rumbles beneath us. The rain becomes a torrent. I hope the weather deters the helicopter, but it's still there, trailing us. And the sirens from the cars I'd been trying to block out wail behind us. The sky darkens, the cloud thick and brooding. We're near the coast now, I can see the sea in the distance.

I hit a wall of terror. Panic paralyses me. I'm going to die whether I get off the bike or stay on it. My heart pounds, juddering through me. I feel it like the wing, the eagle wing, trying to escape my body. And suddenly I'm flying. I watch my human form below on the bike, yet I'm not there, I'm rising skyward. My eyes scan the coast road, the cars menacing behind and the sea being whipped up by the storm. There are cliffs ahead. I fly out over them, the waves crashing into the rock below. My heart is released. I know what to do.

Gil brings the bike to a halt. I'm back in my body. We're a hundred metres from the cliff edge. The wind buffets us and the rain batters down. He pulls off his helmet; he'll be free of that, and I join him. His dark hair clings to the side of his face; our clothes and skin are drenched.

He turns to me. 'Now you get off, Dominic.'

'No.'

'Dominic, I'm not taking you over that cliff with me.'

A light suddenly blinds us from the helicopter above. It takes a moment to adjust. They know too. It's the end; we're done. They're probably filming it all – maybe it's being streamed live on a news channel.

'I'm not getting off, Gil,' I say firmly. 'Just drive hard enough to get us beyond the rocks. I'm not scared, not of the sea. I can breathe underwater.'

'Get off, Dominic!' he cries. 'The bike probably won't make it beyond the rocks. It will be better for me, a quicker end, if it doesn't.'

'No.' I shake my head.

'Get off the fucking bike!' he screams.

I won't back down, but I'm crying. It's desperate. 'Get us beyond the rocks, and I'll see you on the other side.'

He's trembling. I don't know if it's from rage or fear or exasperation.

'I'll save you,' I promise him. His face is streaked with water. I can't tell if there are tears, I can only feel my own. 'I'm not leaving you, Gil. That's my choice. I won't surrender, and you can't make me.'

I stare at him. His eyes are fathomless.

'I can't fight you,' he whispers. Something is understood. He glances up at the helicopter and I grip his body again. He revs the engine. He lowers his left hand behind him, towards me. I grip it, our fingers entwining. It's only for seconds, but it's enough. And then, because we're about to charge off a cliff, he raises his hand that's just held mine and makes the victory sign with his fingers. It's a beautiful act. I smile.

His hand explodes. A bullet rips through it. I scream; his blood and flesh spatter my face. He is silent. I do not know how he stays silent. He revs the engine to full throttle, only his right hand controlling the bike now, and then he releases us. We charge forward.

The world slows. The bike swerves and I realise he will probably not get it beyond the rocks now. But I made my choice. I die with him. His body will be the last one I touch. His spirit the one I die with. The cliff edge draws closer. I brace myself for the fall to come and we take off. The bike goes through the air. I spread my arms wide like I have wings. I will make it beyond the rocks.

Then I'm tumbling through the sky. Flailing. I hit the water hard. The current sucks me under, taking me down into the sea's depths. And I'm drowning. My lungs fill. I can't breathe underwater anymore. Fear and panic course through me, I won't get to the surface in time. But bubbles rise from my lips. I'm still breathing, I can do it. I just have to control my panic. My mind clears: I need to find Gil. If I'm struggling, he'll be dying. I dive down where the water is calmer and swim back towards the shore. He must be near the rocks. I'm lighter than him and the bike propelled me further forward. But if he's on the rocks …

I see his body. He's not struggling to swim, but I won't say he's dead either. I reach him. His body is heavy with sodden clothes and I fight to get him to the surface. Then his face is above water and I need to get us to the shore. I look up. The helicopter is circling but the wind is fierce, the waves high. Surely there's nothing for them to see? At last, it withdraws. It drifts into the distance and then it's gone. Gil and I are alone.

The sea is powerful and despair wells up and crashes down on me with the waves; they take us forward then suck us back. I try again and again to swim to shore until finally the beach is a painful bed of rock and stone beneath us. I pass out for a while. When I wake the storm is cloaking us with its freezing, numbing wind and rain.

I move to Gil. He is pale, a sickly kind of colour. I touch him.

'Gil,' I beg. There's no response. No flicker of an eyelid, no spasm in his limbs. I feel for his pulse but I don't know what I'm feeling. He may be dead. No! I yank his head back and take the only action I can. I put my mouth to his and breathe into him. I sit back a moment, take a breath myself then breathe into him again. I do it three, four times. Still no response. I'm frantic.

'Gil. Come back!'

I breathe into him a fifth time. He coughs, water spurts from his mouth and he's choking. He turns on his side, half breathing, half vomiting water then he's gasping for air. His eyes are wild, he can barely focus, but he's alive. I dare to glance at his left hand. It's gone but for some skin and bone, it's a smashed-up mess. He needs help. And I'm freezing. I hadn't realised till now how cold I am.

'Charley,' I whisper, but my tongue is numb. I want her here, my twin, but she'll be hundreds of miles away.

'*Charley!*' my thoughts scream. We only communicate through our thoughts when we're in the same room, but still I call her now. I might die despite all my effort. '*Charley!*' my thoughts are louder, desperate. *I'm sorry, please forgive me. Let me know if I die you forgive me?*' I lie back exhausted on the shingle.

'*Dominic.*' I hear her, but I'm so cold and exhausted I realise it's a hallucination. Perhaps this happens as you slip towards death? I try to raise my head a little to look out over the sea. Maybe I'll see her or Mary walking across the water? That would be a comfort if it's the last thing I see.

'*Do – min – ic!*' Her voice is loud, forceful. I understand; it's not a hallucination.

'*Charley, we're alive. We need help.*'

Silence. Second after second. Then I hear her.

'*Hold on, we think we know where you are. They're working it out from the news.*'

I whimper. This may soon be over. Gil is very still, but his chest rises and falls.

'They're coming,' I whisper, or perhaps I'm talking to him in my head. I no longer know. 'Don't die now.'

CHAPTER 34

There are faces above me. Charley, Flint and Baz. I think I'm dreaming but I feel too cold to be asleep. I try to focus, there are others here too. I didn't hear them arrive. They attend to Gil first. He moans. I hate the sound of it but they think that's a good sign. Charley's hand touches my face. I see it but can't feel it.

'You're freezing,' a woman tells me. 'Hypothermia. But we'll get you warm. Have you broken anything?'

I try to shake my head, no.

'No serious gashes or cuts?'

Again, I shake my head.

'Baz,' Charley says. 'We need to give them evidence that he's dead. I want to take his clothes. I'll swim out to sea and leave them there.'

The three of them hover around me. I'm so glad they're there.

Baz nods. 'Yeah, that sounds good. Flint, help me out.'

Baz and Flint start unzipping and pulling at my clothes. They're wet and stick to me; removing them is not a gentle process, but they persevere. Then Charley gathers them up.

'I didn't authorise this,' Tom's voice intrudes.

'We can take Gil's clothes too,' Flint says.

'I didn't authorise this,' Tom repeats, sternly.

'You said it's important they believe Dom is dead,' Flint says. 'That they probably know he can breathe underwater so we have to do something convincing.' He's edging towards defiance. There is an uncomfortable silence then Flint placates him. 'But it's your choice.'

'Let's do it, man.' Baz looks across at Tom. 'It's the best evidence we can provide other than his body.'

'Probably,' Tom concedes. 'Go then. We still need time to stabilise Gil but, Charley, be quick. We're not delaying getting out of here because you're frolicking in the water.'

Charley doesn't reply, but the threat is clear. She turns from him and with her arms full she walks quickly into the sea. It's freezing water but she doesn't hesitate. She plunges in and disappears from view.

They wrap me in what looks like tinfoil. 'It's a space blanket,' someone tells me. 'When we get you to the van we'll get you warmer.' I'm shivering again. They smile at that.

Time distorts, everything seems to go on too long. They haul us up off the shore to the coast above. But Charley's not back. The doors to a white van are opened and we all get inside. I don't know how so many people can fit in. It feels hard to breathe, claustrophobic.

I try to sit up. 'You can't go without Charley.'

'Stay cool,' Baz says. 'I'm going to wait for her. We've got this van and a couple of bikes.'

'I'll come with you,' Flint says quickly.

'Sit down.' Tom turns on Flint.

'I'm not leaving Charley.'

'Flint,' Baz says firmly. 'You do as Tom says. I'll take care of Charley.'

Baz steps away from the van and the doors are closed. It's dark, airless. The last time I was in the back of a truck with the Disciples, I'd been shot. We were also running for our lives. The memory closes in, I feel it in my body.

'Keep your nerve, Dominic,' Tom says. He remembers too. He was cruel to me then, and I don't expect much more now.

Then we're off. We travel for a while in silence. There are two women and another man in the truck with us. They must be uncomfortable, squeezed up against the walls of the vehicle. Gil and I are lying down.

'Don't leave us, Gil,' Tom says softly. 'Whatever you do, don't leave us.'

Gil doesn't even moan in response. He could die, that possibility is very real.

The van comes to a halt. I open my eyes, I must have fallen asleep. Tom speaks slowly. 'Get out quietly, no talking, and go into the gamekeeper's lodge. Then Eli and I will take Gil up to the mansion.'

I listen. Is it possible we're back at the mansion house we all lived in before? I was never taken to a gamekeeper's lodge but there probably was one on the estate. That means we're in the Highlands.

'I don't know how safe we are,' Tom says. 'Times have changed. But ... our *landowner friend* has offered us this. I want to believe he's still true to the cause, but we can never know who might betray us. We can't afford to drop our guard. Keep your firearms close at all times.'

There is a communal murmur. The doors to the van open. I don't have the strength to move but Flint and one of the women carry me into the lodge, an old cottage with a quaint garden. The musty smell hits me immediately; the place hasn't been inhabited for years. The ceilings are low, the lights dim. Then I'm lying on cold tiles in a small kitchen until they carry me to a bed. A bare mattress and pillow. Flint comes back with blankets. He throws them over me and tucks them in tight. Our eyes meet. I know he's not happy that Charley's not with us. None of us wanted any of this, but we stick together; he'll look after me. At last, I'm safe enough to sleep.

When I wake, I'm warm, and it's the most comforting sensation. My eyes and ears gradually adjust to my new environment, the gamekeeper's lodge. I look around the small room. There is another bed near mine. Someone's slept in it and I recognise Flint's T-shirt lying on the pillow. I try to sit up but my muscles scream. I've never felt so stiff, my whole body is clenched. I wait a while. I think of calling for help but decide against it; Tom is probably here.

Eventually, I manage to get up and leave the room. The cottage is small and I walk to the living room where I hear the murmur of voices. Rolled-up sleeping bags rest against the wall. Flint is sitting on a sofa with the woman they called Eli. Baz is sprawled out in the armchair.

'Hey, you're up,' Flint says, seeing me. He manages to smile.

'Where's Charley?' I ask, anxious.

'Charley's with Gemma,' Baz says. 'There was a change of plan.'

Flint looks across at me and nods, although I don't think he's happy about it.

'I don't understand,' I say. Gemma has a child, she kept herself apart.

'We decided it was safer if you're in separate locations,' Baz says. 'Charley's cool with it. Gemma's place is a less … military environment.'

I consider trying to speak to Charley through my thoughts, but I don't have the energy. And maybe we won't be able to do that again; it only happened because the situation was so extreme. I have to trust Baz.

'You okay?' Flint asks softly.

I nod.

'Charley's okay too,' he says, but I sense he's saying it to himself as much as to me. He must be missing her.

'And Gil?' I ask, unsure I can take the answer.

'Gil's alive,' Baz says. 'They had to amputate his hand and some of his lower arm, but he's … he should pull through.'

I suddenly feel faint and lean against the doorpost. Gil's lost his hand. 'But he's not in hospital,' I say, knowing that's not possible. He'd be arrested immediately.

'No, he's up at the mansion. They had to do it there. It was makeshift, but he survived.'

I close my eyes. I feel sick.

'You should take it easy,' Eli says, watching me. I notice her short-cropped dark hair, tattoos on her arms, and the pistol in a holster around her shoulder.

I go back to the bedroom and lie down again. I'm shaking. I remember my dream like a horror movie, the one with the eagle wing where I lost my arm. I clench the blankets. It's not me, but Gil.

CHAPTER 35

Tom and I sit alone in the kitchen. He opens his laptop on the table.

'Time to catch up on your obituaries,' he says without emotion.

This is the first time I've looked at the news. I've spent days sleeping. It's also my first time alone with Tom. A few days ago we fought, and I'm not challenging his authority again.

We were all in the living room and I asked if I could see Gil.

'Gil needs time and space to recover,' Tom said. 'He can't be worrying about you. If you've got anything you need to say, you can say it to me.'

'I need to see him,' I said, because the need felt like a burning pain.

'Don't push me, Dominic,' Tom warned.

'Gil and I went through something together and I have to see him.'

'Dominic, remember why you're here and how much you fucking owe us. I'm in charge now and you obey me. You will not be seeing Gil and you don't ask again.'

Later, Baz said. 'Everyone's upset, Tom too. We have to stay cool with each other.'

Now, I'm working very hard at staying cool. Neither Flint nor I have any idea when we'll see Charley again, and they're in complete control. I sit with Tom and we scroll through newspaper articles, watch the recorded footage of the chase, and gauge what's gone viral on social media. There seems to be an endless appetite for watching Gil lose his hand and then viewing us going over that cliff.

'It's gruesome,' I say, shocked. 'I don't get how anyone can want to watch it.'

'Because human beings like to explore life's extremes – vicariously, of course.'

I shake my head, upset.

'The good news though is you're dead,' Tom says. 'They think Gil is too, although … we'll correct them on that in due course. But for the moment, a dead revolutionary has his own particular power. Those who admire us, who may not even like us, but privately admire us, are sharing picture after picture of Gil.'

Each link we click on shows Gil with his hand raised in the victory sign, an image he's given many a security camera. They've been viewed millions of times.

'It's like he's a celebrity,' I say, staggered at what's happened.

'Yes. This goes beyond anything we could have wished for.' Tom smiles. 'And people are drawn to this story too, because of the sacrifice of you and him for what you believe in.'

'Sacrifice?' I query. I scan the lines of news, and we play an interview recorded with Magda. She stands before the camera insisting she knew nothing, she's bewildered.

'They think I'm the victim of a dangerous, manipulative man,' I say. 'Someone who's much better dead than alive.'

Tom laughs. 'They have to say that. But …' he goes back to an image of Gil, his dark eyes defiant, his hand in a V sign, 'this is what people remember.'

I can't sleep. I lie awake staring at the ceiling. Flint is snoring in the other bed. Over dinner, Tom and Baz were tense. I decided not to ask why. If they're afraid for our safety, I don't want to know. There is nowhere else to go. I realise we might all be shot, like my father was, but I've run out of fear.

A car draws up outside, I hear its doors open and close. There is the sound of footsteps then voices, almost a commotion, coming from the hallway. The voices dull a little; whoever has arrived must have gone into the kitchen. I sit up slowly and leave the bedroom. The kitchen door is ajar, a brief sliver of light falling across the otherwise dark hallway. I move towards it to listen. I recognise a familiar voice – Gemma. If she's here, does that mean my sister is too?

'Of course I've taken precautions,' she says sharply. 'And don't forget, nobody looks at me and sees a Disciple, it wouldn't cross their mind. I'm just a harassed mother with a kid screaming in the back of the car and my *cousin* here helping out.'

Charley must be with her.

'It's another layer of risk,' Tom says coolly.

'Listen, I've sat tight. I've swallowed every instinct in me so that I stay away, but now …' Her voice starts to crack. 'Babe,' she whispers, softening, 'we both know that before my child was born we didn't know if it would be yours or Gil's. And if it had been yours, wouldn't you want to see your son before you died?'

There is a tense moment's silence. I've stopped breathing.

'Nobody said Gil's dying,' Tom says slowly.

'Honey, do you think I don't understand what you're telling me when you say he's deteriorating?' Again, a pause. 'Let me see him. I need to say goodbye.'

I have to lean against the hallway wall. I'm shaking. And then I hear Charley. 'I'm not prepared to be away from Flint and Dom anymore.' There are a few footsteps, the kitchen door opens and Charley walks out. She sees me and her expression tells me to retreat. I move quickly back to the bedroom and close the door behind us. I hug her quickly. I feel her hands grip the back of my neck.

'I've missed you,' I whisper. 'I've missed you, Charley. And I'm sorry, for everything I got wrong. I'm sorry, I'm sorry, I'm sorry.'

Her nails are digging into me as she hugs me tighter.

Flint wakes. 'Hey!'

We shush him quickly. Charley goes to hug him. She pushes him back on the bed so her whole body can wrap around his. She's crying now.

'Hey,' he says softly. 'I love you too. Charley, Charley.'

We take a few minutes to calm down. I sit opposite them on my bed.

'Is Gil dying?' I ask.

Charley shrugs. 'I'm not sure what's happening. The whole situation has been doing Gemma's head in. She's just wanted to be with him, and earlier, she got this call saying he was deteriorating and that was it.'

I can't speak. I don't want to admit how upset I am.

'And Benjamin, her baby,' Charley says, 'he looks so like Gil, it's freaky. And she says he's crying much more than he usually does, he knows something's wrong. And to be honest, his crying was getting to me. I'm glad to get away from them.'

Flint puts his arm around her shoulder and squeezes her tight.

She drops her voice. 'Dom, you need to be careful. They … they're starting to blame you for Gil. I mean not just you, but also Gil. They think he made an error, a serious error of judgement in not leaving you behind. I couldn't say anything to Gemma, it was too dangerous, but she's been confiding in me. She's afraid they'll try to oust him as their leader. At the very least they'll discipline him.'

I'm stunned. 'That's insane. Gil *is* the Disciples. They can't exist without him.'

'All I know is there's a lot of bad feeling going around and we need to keep our heads down.'

I can't believe what's happening. 'But Tom and Baz have said nothing.'

'Do you think they'd be discussing it with you?' Charley asks.

I'm speechless. Gil might be dying and they're turning on him. How can that be right?

Flint shakes his head. 'None of it surprises me.'

'But what about us?' I ask.

'We've got to watch our backs,' Charley whispers. 'For the moment, I think we're safe. We're too valuable to lose but … Tom doesn't like you, Dom. Even Gemma was saying things that …' She stops. Her eyes hold mine. 'You should have told us what you were doing and about Justin.'

'Yeah. I should have.'

'I knew something was wrong, I begged you to confide in me, but you didn't trust us.'

'Of course I trusted you,' I say quickly. 'I … I just didn't want to tell you things I thought you wouldn't want to hear. And I thought I could get that information for Dad. I just wanted to complete something for him.'

'I've been away from you enough days to forgive you, Dom. But …' Her voice drops even lower. 'Dad … Dad was a Disciple. You could never have done what you wanted on your own – you should have left it to them. You need never have got involved, and you should never have kept it from us. That's what hurts, because if you'd told us, we'd have insisted you left it to them.'

'Charley, you can say that now but you've hated the Disciples. You'd never have told me to leave it to them.'

'I would. What I feel about them wouldn't have mattered – it would have been about what I know they can do.'

I can't talk about it anymore. I don't believe she would have said that, but I understand she wants to make sense

189

of what's happened. I lie back on my bed, exhausted again. Charley curls up next to Flint. We try and get some sleep.

Later, I wake, hot and thirsty. I walk softly down to the kitchen to get a glass of water. Gemma is sitting there in the dark and silence. Her blouse is open and her bra. Her left nipple is half in, half out of her baby's mouth. He's fallen asleep. She's stroking his head gently. She turns to me.

'Your son,' I whisper, 'he's very like Gil.'

She smiles. 'Yes, surprising how such a young child can look like someone who's lived for years.'

I ask carefully, 'Will he … do you think Gil will live?' I swallow, aware I only want to hear one answer.

'I hope so,' she says, but not in a way that sounds hopeful.

I get myself a glass of water and give her one too. Then I sit down opposite her.

'I'm sorry,' I say, because she's sad.

'Yes.'

Silence spreads between us. I can feel her upset, it hangs in the air.

'If you had been a braver person,' she says softly, 'you would have surrendered. You would have released Gil because he could have escaped without going over a cliff if you'd stayed behind.'

Her words are a punch in the stomach.

'I love Gil,' she says, 'but he made a – possibly fatal – error of judgement. And you were a part of it.'

My lower lip trembles. I want to tell her no, she's not being fair, but I can't speak.

'I keep thinking how if Charley hadn't insisted she was sure you were alive, if they'd not found you on the beach as they did, both you and Gil might be dead now. Would … would that have been its own justice?'

'Gemma,' I say, but then I have to stop. It's hard to breathe. 'I never wanted any of this to happen.'

'Of course not, but it has.'

'I-I didn't ask Gil to take me.'

'But you didn't offer to stay either.'

I'm shivering. My voice is choked. It takes me a while to stand up and walk out. Gemma doesn't say anything else. I'd always thought she was kind, one of the better ones among them, but her words feel like a bullet in my chest.

CHAPTER 36

I fly. Mary comes to me in my dream and tells me to get out of there. To rise up, to fly off; I don't belong to them. I think this time I'll do it, I'll fly to the mountains. I'll leave them all behind. I watch the gamekeeper's lodge diminish below me, and then I head out. The mansion house isn't so far away, not when you're flying. I circle it. I call out to him, surprised at the sound. An eagle's cry: sharp, decisive. He should hear me. He should know; he did when I willed him not to leave me. 'Survive,' I order. I command. 'Survive.'

'Dom, wake up.' Flint shakes my shoulder. 'It's lunchtime.'

I open my eyes. 'I can't move.'

'Of course you can,' he says.

I shake my head. 'I'm not moving.' I miss lunch.

Charley comes in. 'Dom, what's going on?'

I just shake my head. Can't tell her.

'*Don't block me out of your thoughts,*' she whispers into my head.

'*I'm blocking everything out,*' I tell her.

I lie there silent, miserable.

'*Gemma's gone,*' she says.

I sit up slowly. 'Really?'

She nods.

'She said things …' I stop. Charley's quiet. 'Am I a coward?' I ask.

'No, Dom, you're not that.' I think she's just being kind.

'Because I can see,' I say, 'that I fuck up and then you, Flint, Gil … you all take the heat for what I've done.'

She doesn't answer immediately then says softly, 'Flint thinks if MI5 had decided to pick us up weeks ago, which they could have, we'd be locked up now without hope. So talking about where you went wrong, or what you did with Justin, is irrelevant. He was MI5. Everything was already out of our control.'

'Flint said that?' I sense he's forgiving me.

'Yeah, he's really been thinking about things.'

I'm still. 'But Gil got hurt. Maybe I could have stopped that happening?'

'*Dom, get real. Gil getting hurt is inevitable. He's the leader of a terrorist group.*'

I take a deep breath, aware that's probably true.

'Listen,' she says aloud, sitting on the bed by me. 'The hardest thing we've got to deal with is the truth about what Dad did to us. What that might mean.'

'I can't think about it,' I say quickly. 'Can hardly think beyond the next minute or the next hour. It's for another time, Charley.'

Our eyes meet. Her expression is hard to read.

'We have each other,' I say softly. 'We'll get our heads around it, and … we don't have to face it alone.'

'I'd like to believe that one day I'll have a home, I'll feel safe somewhere.'

'Charley, you will.' I've no idea what the truth will be for me, but I know she will have that.

She gets up to leave the room and this time I follow.

Days pass and something's changing. Tom and Baz withdraw from me. When I enter a room, they leave it. When we're all eating together in the kitchen, they avoid my eyes.

They don't share any new information. I'm on edge; it's not a good sign.

And then Tom tells me. 'Dominic, tomorrow night we're having an inquiry into everything that happened. You'll come to the kitchen at eight where a team of us will interview you.'

'An inquiry?'

'It's normal procedure after a significant event or major operation.'

'Did you have one after Operation Gideon?' I ask, because I was a key player and nobody ever spoke to me about it afterwards.

'Naturally.' Tom nods, but his eyes are cold. I don't feel comfortable at all.

I enter the kitchen at eight on the dot. The room is crowded and tense. Tom sits centre stage at the table, his eyes focused on me. Baz sits on his right side and Eli on his left. Their expressions are cold, officious. Next to Baz is another woman who's introduced as Kat. Her dark hair is tied back in a tight ponytail and there's a scar below her right eye. Next to Eli sits Gil. Gil. I'm shocked. I didn't expect him to be here. His face is pale and there are dark circles around his eyes. His left arm is in a sling, a huge sling; I imagine him bound and bandaged within it. He was always slim but now he's too thin. I sense he's in pain but his face is impassive. Compared to the others, he seems small, wounded. I know immediately that none of this is going to be fair. Gil's on the edge of them, he's not controlling events.

'Sit down,' Tom says, indicating the chair opposite him.

I sit but the more I'm aware of Gil's presence, the sicker I feel. I've wanted to see him but not like this.

Tom starts the proceedings. 'Before you phoned us, seeking our help, what was the last contact you had with Gil?'

I pause a moment, unsure what's happening. 'He wrote to me after my father's death,' I say quietly.

'And in that letter he told you that we, the Disciples, would avenge your father's death?'

'Yes.'

'What did you do with that letter?'

'I burnt it,' I say truthfully.

'To destroy the evidence? Or because you didn't like its content?'

Do I lie or do I tell the truth? Something in me is determined to tell the truth. 'Both. I felt very angry towards you all. You freed my father and then he was murdered anyway.' I'm being interrogated like I'm a criminal, but they're the ones who messed up.

'Is that why you were happy to act alone, acquiring what you thought would be relevant information from Justin Pendleton?'

'Yes, that's exactly why I decided to act alone.'

'Did you at any point think of approaching us with that information, or informing us of what you were doing?'

I hesitate a moment. 'I … I always knew it was possible, if I felt I'd got in out of my depth, I knew I could go back to Gil.'

'You knew you could go back to Gil,' Tom says slowly. 'You went back to Gil, didn't you, when we freed your father?'

I nod. They already know this; he's not asking me these questions because he needs answers. Where's this all going?

'Do you consider yourself a Disciple?' he asks easily.

My shoulders tighten, I need to be careful. 'In the eyes of the law I am, after Operation Gideon.'

'In the eyes of the law, Dominic, there is no doubt you'd be convicted as a Disciple, but I'm asking you how you think of yourself. Where your … loyalty lies?'

'Sometimes …' I say softly, 'I think of myself as a Disciple.'

'Sometimes. Is that loyalty?' he asks, but not like he wants an answer.

My eyes scan them all quickly. I would like to avoid looking at Gil but I can't. He's very still; his expression reveals nothing.

'Given your degree of loyalty,' Tom says coolly, 'do you think when you left us and Gil threatened to shoot you, but didn't, that he made the right judgement?'

Nothing could have prepared me for that. A shiver runs through my body. This isn't about recent events. My mouth is dry. I glance at Gil. His face still shows nothing. Tom must really hate me.

'Do you?' I ask, but my voice is almost inaudible.

'I'm asking the questions, Dominic. Not you.'

'Of course I think he made the right judgement,' I say, my throat tight. 'If not I'd be dead.'

'Yes,' he says quietly, 'and we'd have fewer problems.'

I'm speechless. I think it's possible, even after everything that's happened, that they might kill me.

'Why do you think he let you go, Dominic?'

I'm silent. My breath quickens.

'I would suggest, Dominic, that with you Gil lacks the judgement he normally shows. He let you leave us, which was a considerable risk after Operation Gideon. And then, again, after you recently sought our help and brought MI5 to us, he made an even graver error of judgement. He took you with him. None of us doubts he would have evaded them on his own, and kept his hand.'

I can't look at Gil. I can barely look at any of them. I can't believe what's happening. Tom is Gil's friend. He's the Disciples' second in command. They were always close. Why is he doing this?

'They're not the judgements a leader should make,' Tom says.

I'm shaking. I'm sitting there and I can't control the shaking in my body. I have no idea how this is going to end, only it's not going to be good for me. And probably not Gil.

I didn't think the Disciples were capable of anything more ruthless or cruel than I'd already experienced, but they are. Will they get Gil to shoot me now?

'This is your opportunity to speak.' Tom sits back.

I swallow hard, my thoughts scrambling; I have to say something. 'I think G-G-Gil made the right judgements,' I stammer. I pause. My mouth is so dry. 'If he'd shot me, the seventeen-year-old son of the loyal Disciple, Brian Minster …' A wave of nausea crashes over me. 'If he'd done that … it would have been so brutal and cruel, it would have cancelled out everything the Disciples stand for.' I pause again, grasping what I need to say. 'Gil acts with his conscience and …' I take a deep breath, 'his heart. And without that, the Disciples are nothing. Revolutionaries, warriors, whatever word you want to use, they destroy what they stand for when they get too brutal – they just alienate. So Gil made the right judgement of a leader who stands for something … who people admire.' I stop, but then continue because I can't keep the words down. 'And he didn't leave me behind, Tom, because he's brave. I couldn't figure out why anyone would keep watching us going over that cliff, but I get it now. You watch that footage, and it's clear Gil's telling me to get off the bike – but I don't. People are fascinated because they don't know that kind of courage and commitment themselves, but they can see Gil and I have it for each other. And it's powerful. It's what a leader inspires. And that's Gil.'

I finish. I can't look at them. I had no idea I was going to say those things until they came out. The room is silent. I've spoken the truth and I'm rattling as a result. I've no idea what they'll do to me.

'Great answer,' Baz says softly. I raise my eyes and he smiles at me. Tom swallows. Eli and Kat look ashamed. And Gil's eyes are fire. Thank God, he's still there.

'Perhaps now,' Gil says slowly, calmly, 'we can focus on the task in hand. Avenging Brian Minster's death and releasing the necessary information.' He may be physically depleted but his voice is strong.

I'm dismissed from the room as they continue their discussion. I crash out on my bed, my face buried in my pillow. After a while, Charley and Flint come in.

'It may not surprise you,' Flint says quietly, 'but we heard every word.' I turn over onto my side to face them. 'For a moment,' he says, 'I thought I was gonna have to come in there and save you.' We both know he couldn't have done that. ''Cause, shit, that got scary.'

I slowly turn my eyes to my sister. 'I know you don't understand,' I say. 'Not about Gil. You'll never see him like I do.' She is quiet. 'But, some of the most extreme moments in my life, and the most intense feelings I've had, have happened with Gil. And that does something to you. You just feel connected.' I take a few deep breaths.

'I understand … some of it,' she says gently.

'He looks like shit. He's really been hurt.'

'Yeah,' Flint says. 'Just the moment for his so-called comrades, his "brothers and sisters" to turn on him.'

'I felt sick walking into that room. And when I saw him …' I shake my head. 'I don't know how they could do that.'

'Power,' Flint says under his breath. 'It's always about people wanting power.'

CHAPTER 37

Baz sets up the camera, focusing the lens on me. I fidget where I sit. I've never done anything like this before.

'Remember,' he says, 'what we're creating is a film made weeks ago, maybe even months ago, you can't reference anything recent.'

'But you want me to be honest?' I check.

'About your dad, about what he told you, even about us, yes.'

He starts recording. 'We can do as many takes as we need.' He smiles encouragingly.

I stare at the lens. I've no idea how many people will eventually watch this, but it could be a lot.

'I never wanted to be a Disciple,' I say slowly. 'I never wanted to have anything to do with them, but my father's actions changed that. I need to tell you the truth because nobody else is. I was a sixteen-year-old schoolkid when this started. I lived in a lovely home and my dad, he was a good father. He lost everything because he wanted to tell the truth. So you can ask yourself, as you hear this, as you maybe question it, why would a man give up everything he had, owned and loved? Because the truth matters, and they don't want you to know about it, not the government or LifeStar Corporation or any of those people invested in this project. But what I'm about to tell you is not just about me or my father or the Disciples. It's about you. And what could happen to you.'

In all, I speak for three minutes. I never mention the secret of my own genes. I stick to telling people what's being done with the information about theirs. I don't know how I come across, I'm too close to it all, but Baz seems satisfied. He says it's part of an overall package they're putting together.

The following day, they go through interviews recorded with my father, putting together segments of the most important points. I can hear it playing in the kitchen. Flint and Charley are in there, but I keep my distance. What Dad wanted is coming to fruition; this will soon be over, and I'm missing Mary. I know MI5 will have interviewed her and Gregory. How do I apologise for the difficulties I've caused them? I want to believe she knows I'm still alive; she's part of why I'm still alive. But it's not like I can write her a letter or just pop by. And once our work with the Disciples is done, where will we go? They've told us they're working on that too, ensuring we disappear. How will I get back to Mary?

It takes over a week to put everything together and to agree on how they'll distribute it. The eight-minute film will be streamed on every available portal. All the national papers and broadcasters will be sent a transcript and receive a copy of the letter Justin gave me.

'It doesn't matter that it's a set-up,' Tom says. 'They would always deny it was real, even if it were. The point is it contains enough of the truth.' He's more normal now, the loyal colleague, Gil's worthy second in command.

'And then what?' I ask.

'Then it's up to the rest of society to make its decision. We'll have vindicated what your father did, and we'll have provided as much information as possible.'

'You … you suggested at one point,' I say carefully, 'that you could take out the Kendrick facility.'

Tom smiles. 'Oh, we'll enjoy doing that.'

We sit as a group in the kitchen and watch the fruit of our labours on Tom's laptop. It starts with me, and the message I recorded in case I should die, which I have now. I sound young and angry and then upset. It's followed by the recordings of my father, with pictures of him with work colleagues, LifeStar's main office, maps, and DNA patterns shown as a montage while he speaks. Then there's a brief piece where Gil addresses the camera. It's obvious he's still recovering, but the look in his eyes, the determination on his face and in his voice is absolute. I'm reminded again of how much Gil believes and believes completely in what he stands for; it's his strength and power. His conviction draws you in. His voice is clear and strong.

'Dominic Minster was a true warrior. His death should be mourned by everyone.' He talks of my father and the need for justice and truth. How people are made to believe they have small lives and they give their power away to governments, institutions and companies.

'Your data, your biological inheritance, is being used to create this weapon. Ask for it back. Demand it. Deny those who would survey you, monitor you, manipulate you.'

His speech is short, but proof that he's alive and kicking. It ends with him raising his right hand in the victory sign. The Disciples will not be defeated. I wonder when I'll see him again in person.

His image fades, the film ends and the screen goes blank. Everyone is silent, taking in the overall effect of the film.

'It's powerful,' Tom says.

'Yeah.' Baz nods. 'Happy with it?' He turns to me.

I take a moment to respond. 'It will produce a reaction, won't it?' It's hitting home how something that's been so powerfully personal, and about my father, will be in the public domain. All of it. It's shocking.

'Yeah, that's what we want. A reaction,' Tom says, satisfied.

Sunday evening it goes out. It's when you'd least expect such information to hit the internet, but it also ensures everyone's talking about it when they go into work on Monday. The newspaper editors have time to put it on their front pages, and just before midnight there's a government announcement: there will be a Cabinet Office Security Briefing in the morning.

The reaction is swift and immediate. I didn't expect it to be so vicious. We sit in the kitchen flicking through articles and between TV channels on the several laptops before us. The Disciples are accused of excelling themselves as enemies of the state. They're liars and criminals who've released information that can only harm the nation and provide succour to our potential enemies.

'The Russians will love this,' one minister is quoted as saying.

The government tries to deny it, but people are making their own minds up. Peace campaigners are camping outside the Ministry of Defence and in the media and online a swathe of voices is congratulating the Disciples for bringing this important truth to light.

LifeStar Corporation releases a statement denying they've ever been involved in such a project. All their genetic research is for the betterment of humanity. Brian Minster was a man who had become mentally ill and deluded, and their only regret was not having insisted he seek treatment earlier. Security guards at their head office push journalists aside as they try to interview employees entering the building. I wonder what Ian Pendleton thinks of it all? If he still has his job.

We eat our evening meal with our thoughts on the news rather than our food.

'What if,' I ask slowly, 'what if what we've done isn't enough, the voices of the establishment block out the truth, and nothing changes?'

Everyone grows quiet.

'We can control the information we put out there,' a voice says gently behind me, 'but we can't control how people receive it, or ultimately, what they do about it.'

We all turn to the doorway. It's Gil. It's the first time I've seen him since the 'inquiry'. He looks a lot better than he did then. His face has colour, he's put on a little weight, but his arm is still in a sling.

Tom stands and goes over to greet him. They give each other a half hug to avoid touching Gil's left arm. Baz then rises and finally Eli, each greeting him in turn.

'It's good to have you back,' Baz says. Tom gets a chair for Gil to sit by him.

Charley, Flint and I are silent. I don't know what to say when it feels like there is everything I want to say.

'We've done the best we can,' Gil says, his eyes on us. 'The thing with knowledge is when people hear things that are difficult to hear, like this is, they respond in different ways: denying it, being outraged, taking action, or hoping it will just go away. Perhaps like you felt, Dominic, when all this started.'

'But,' I say, 'it didn't go away.'

'No,' Gil acknowledges. 'And deep down, the government, LifeStar Corporation, and even the general public know this isn't going away either. What we've done is only the beginning, it was always part of a much bigger battle. Your father knew that, that's why he came to us.'

'Has it been worth it?' Charley asks, her voice quiet. 'Dad's dead. You lost Riley. It's cost so much in different ways.' She gazes at Gil's left arm. 'It's not possible to get any of that back and …' She sounds more sad than angry.

'Your father never doubted it was worth it,' Gil says softly. 'There are times when doubt has a valuable purpose, but not now.'

There is a short period of quiet then Gil turns to me. 'I'd like to speak to you alone, Dominic.'

CHAPTER 38

Gil and I leave the kitchen. We go to the bedroom where it's private. He closes the door behind him. We are alone and it's the strangest feeling. After going through something so intense and terrifying together, I'm not sure how to relate to him. Not normally.

He speaks in a whisper. 'Dominic, I know what you did for me. I think I died. I remember knowing I was dying and then … I believe I did, but you somehow brought me back.'

I'm silent.

'I don't know exactly what you did, but … maybe it was something similar to what Charley must have done to you when you were dying of septicaemia.'

I'm speechless. He's been working things out lying in that bed recovering. We were never going to let the Disciples know what Charley was capable of doing. She breathed into me back then, and somehow I survived. But I can't know if I have that ability.

'I always knew you were exceptional,' he says.

'I don't know what I did, Gil. Not really. Only I couldn't let you die. I couldn't lose somebody else, not after Dad.'

'No. I understand …'

'You won't tell anyone, will you?' I ask, because he now knows something that he cannot share.

'No … and thank you. I thank you for saving my life, Dominic.'

'You saved mine. You could have left me. That would have been the better thing for you to do. I can see that. But you didn't. I thank you, too.' I glance at his arm. 'I hate that you got hurt.'

'It's been hard,' he says. 'I'm struggling to accept it, but I will.' I didn't expect him to be so honest.

'Was it an error of judgement?'

He waits a moment. 'No,' he says. Then I hear him in my head, although his lips don't move. '*Having a heart comes at a cost.*'

I freeze. 'Did you just do what I think you did?'

'What?' he asks.

'*Speak into my thoughts,*' I say, silent.

He doesn't reply. 'What?' he repeats. He hasn't heard me. That's a relief. If not …

'I thought … I thought I heard you speak into my mind,' I say carefully.

'Really?' He seems bemused. 'What did you imagine I said?'

'Having a heart comes at a cost.'

'Well, I would agree with that,' he says softly.

I watch him. His eyes are smiling at me.

'Shortly, Dominic, we're going to discuss the plans we've made for you.'

'Okay,' I say, growing nervous.

'We've got you all new identities, and we're going to smuggle you into Europe.'

I listen. 'But I need to go back to Mary.'

'That can't happen and certainly not at the moment.'

I feel panic in my chest. 'I have to go back to her, Gil. She … she in her way saved me.'

'I don't doubt your feelings, Dominic, but I'm telling you what's going to happen. And I'm telling you before we talk as a group. Your safety is my priority, as is Mary and

Gregory's. I don't want you to question my authority, and not in front of the others. Do you understand?'

I breathe deeply. The inquiry has really affected him.

'In time,' he says, 'it's possible you can go back to her, but not now.'

I swallow hard and nod. I have to accept it. Arguing with him will do neither of us any good. 'How can you trust Tom?' I ask.

'He was upset and afraid. People don't always act their best in those circumstances.'

I couldn't sound so philosophical. 'He's your second in command. He should have treated you with more respect.'

Gil nods. 'Possibly.'

'Don't you sometimes … feel lonely?' I ask.

He smiles at me but doesn't answer. He steps back, our conversation coming to an end.

'Will I see you again, Gil,' I ask, 'after you leave tonight?' I don't know if I should try to hug him. If I need to figure out how to say goodbye.

'Hopefully,' he says, and before I can do or say anything else, he opens the bedroom door and we leave the room.

CHAPTER 39

They give each of us a new name, passport and papers. There's also a large envelope of money.

'You leave tonight,' Tom says. 'The weather's good, the tide right, and the sooner you're out of here the better. The boat will take you round the coast of Scotland and England and then head over to France. It's a large and diverse country, you can reinvent yourselves there.'

'But we don't even speak the language,' Flint says, concerned.

'You'll learn,' Tom says.

'Charley and I speak a bit,' I say, although I don't think it's much comfort to Flint. I had no idea we'd be leaving so soon. After weeks of wanting to get out of the lodge, I suddenly feel reluctant to go. But it's not a choice, it's an order.

We go back into the bedroom to look over our new identities.

'I'm Adam Faber,' I say, aware I've got to adjust to my new name.

'I'm Emma Martin,' Charley says with a French inflection. She shrugs.

'And I'm Theo Mason,' Flint says. 'I don't look like Theo Mason.'

'Flint, what does Theo Mason look like?' I ask.

'I don't know, but he's white.'

'Well, this particular Theo isn't.'

'I hate it,' Flint says decisively.

'It's okay,' Charley says. 'You'll get used to it. I think I like Theo.'

'No, I'm going to tell them they've got to change it,' Flint says, determined. 'They can't just go and get us documents with names we've never even heard of let alone asked for, and then expect us to live with them for years, maybe for the rest of our lives.' He's really wound up.

'Flint, we can't start arguing with them now,' I say.

But he's off and out the room. I hear him talking to Baz and then Tom. This is not good; his voice is rising.

'Shut the fuck up,' Tom shouts.

'Stay calm,' Baz says, sounding more placating. 'You don't lose it, man. Hey? Of the three of you, you're the one who stays cool. You stay cool now. Theo's a good name. You can live with it.'

Then I hear Flint crying. He rarely cries and hearing him pulls at my insides. I go and find him in the living room. Tom and Baz look at me and then withdraw; they've made themselves clear so I can sort it out. I sit beside my cousin whose head is in his hands.

'Flint,' I say, resting my hand on his back. 'What's up? I don't understand.'

'I'm tired, Dom. I liked the life we were living. I enjoyed my job. I always think I can take or do anything, I'm strong, but now it feels like ...' He shakes his head. 'I don't want to go to France. I don't want to be called Theo. I don't ...' He trails off. 'I can't do it.'

I look at him, his body shuddering, miserable. Is it possible he may not come with us? Flint has always been there for us, always adapted for us, but he hasn't had much say. I feel a sudden and intense sadness.

'Flint,' I whisper. 'I find it very hard to leave things I love. I can't go to Mary now. I don't want to go to France either, but … I love you, and I want you to come with us.'

He shakes his head again. What can I do? I wait before continuing. 'If you … if you really feel you can't come with us, then we must let you do what it is you want.' I try to hold my voice steady. I know I'm talking as much to myself as him, trying to get my head round the fact we need to be fair to him. 'I understand,' I say slowly. 'And Charley … Charley will too.' If he doesn't come, it will be an incredible loss. I'm not sure how we'll bear it but I know we'll have too.

Flint grows calmer. The tension in his muscles lessens. Maybe he needed to hear that? He's entitled to a choice. We all know it's Charley and me who have to disappear. He could have a more normal life.

'Okay,' I say softly, squeezing his shoulder. 'You think. It's your choice. I will always love you.'

I get up and leave the room. I go back into the bedroom and realise I'm shaking. Charley is wide eyed and silent.

'*What's he going to do?*' she asks.

'*I don't know.*'

I sit beside her, our bodies close. Our bodies that emerged from the womb together. We share the same genetic inheritance, we've always lived together, and now maybe it's just her and me. Twins. Our fate was decided long ago and we've learnt to stop fighting it. I start crying, but Charley's calm. Is that because she knows him more intimately than me? Are there things they've said lying next to each other that means she can accept he might choose to go his own way? It's not such a shock? I've no idea.

I watch the hands on the clock move round. I try to focus on the documents of my new identity, but I'll have plenty of time to absorb them yet. I think about packing before we go, but there isn't really anything to pack. A few toiletries they got us and some other clothes to wear. Instead, I sit back on my bed wondering what any future will look like.

Someone arrives. I glance at the clock. It's nearly five,

but they said we'd be leaving later. I hear a murmur of voices then a door open and close. Footsteps in the hallway, another door opens.

'You have two choices, Flint.' It's Gil. 'You either go with your cousins or you rejoin the Disciples. What we're not going to let you do is wander off on your own right now. It's too dangerous, and a risk we're not prepared to take.'

Charley and I both sit there silent, listening.

'If … if I join you,' Flint says slowly, 'do I get to blow up the Kendrick facility?'

There's a pause. 'Possibly,' Gil says carefully.

'Where will you put me?' Flint asks.

'You'll join a cell, probably in one of the major cities.'

'And Baz, will I get to see him?'

'Not necessarily,' Gil says pointedly. 'Let me be blunt, Flint. I have always thought you'd make a good Disciple. You've got attitude, we like that. But honestly, right now, I don't trust your emotional reactions. I'm not sure that once you've said goodbye to your cousins, you won't wish to be with them within … oh, I give it forty-eight hours. And if that happens, none of us are going to be happy. I suggest you go with them. If you really feel after you've settled somewhere that it's not the life for you, you can come back and join us. But I demand loyalty. Choose to join us when you're sure of that.'

There is a long moment's silence. 'Understand?' Gil asks.

'Yes,' Flint says softly. 'I get it.'

'Good.' We hear Gil leave the room and then the cottage.

Charley and I are quiet. Gil handled that well. I can only admire him; he sees things other people miss. Flint comes back into the bedroom. He doesn't say anything but sits on the end of the bed and flicks through his documents again. He lets out a sigh. 'I'm sorry,' he whispers.

'That's okay,' Charley says. 'You're allowed to lose it.' He looks at her and nods. 'You know,' she says, her voice

211

hushed, 'I meant what I told you, that if you ever need to go, it's okay. I will always love you. It doesn't change that. We're allowed to want different experiences and … to be with other people.' My sister and Flint have spoken about these things. I'm never that wise or calm, not when it comes to relationships.

Flint nods. 'I know.' Then, after a pause, he adds, 'Right now, you're the person I want to be with.'

She nods and smiles.

We're leaving. The three of us get into the back of the truck while Tom and Baz are in the front. It's the first time we've been outside for weeks. We head for the coast. After Flint's outburst, I know we need to keep cool. They're in no mood to entertain our feelings now. They just need us out of the way.

I try not to think how I'm just a few hours from Mary, but soon we'll be a much greater distance apart. I'm leaving the person I love. I'm leaving the country I know. I didn't even get to sit my exam in French, my German was better. For a moment I think it's mad – all mad. We're not going to be able to pull this off. The Disciples have made a mistake. They want us gone and this is the quickest way they can do it.

'*We'll be alright,*' Charley whispers into my head. '*We stick together and we'll be alright.*'

She's trying to comfort me but I look away and close my eyes, afraid I'll cry.

'*You'll find a way back to Mary.*'

My throat aches. I try to stop my thoughts. I try to ignore the grief I feel opening up inside – a big, painful hole. And then I feel my heart. Anguished, responding, thumping. That eagle wing, at least, won't go. Not without me. It can't. I take a few deep breaths. It will find its way home and take me with it. I grow calmer. We'll be at the coast soon. We'll board that boat, and we'll survive.

The truck comes to a halt and we all get down. We walk to the beach across rock and stone. There is a small dinghy waiting for us and, in the darkening night, I can see a larger boat like a fishing vessel further out to sea. Gil is waiting by the dinghy. His left arm is no longer in a sling; it ends below the elbow, his wrist and hand gone, a thick layer of bandage hiding the stump. I try not to look. Another man sits in the dinghy, ready to take us away.

We all stop. It's time to say goodbye. Charley goes first, turning to Tom and Baz. They embrace each other and she goes to Gil. A few words are spoken and a loose hug shared. She gets in the dinghy. Flint goes next. He and Baz hug the longest. Then I say farewell, even Tom is kind, and I walk to Gil. Charley and Flint are both in the dinghy.

Gil and I are face to face. After everything we've gone through I can't believe this is it, goodbye. He embraces me tight with his right arm, and I hug him back. How many times have I gripped his body as his motorbike sped along? How close have we been? And I'm crying. I don't want to leave him, I don't want to go. I'll promise him I'll be a Disciple, I'll do whatever he wants, just don't make us part. But I don't say any of it.

We withdraw a little from each other. My tears keep flowing. He smiles gently but his eyes are sad. 'Go, Dominic,' he says softly. 'Before I change my mind.'

I try to smile, despite crying. He motions with his eyes for me to get into the boat. Still, I can't move. I don't want to leave him. Then he draws me to him and kisses me hard on the forehead, like a father might or a brother, and he pushes me towards the dinghy. I turn and get in. The guy waiting starts to row away. I don't look back. I try to focus on the fishing boat ahead but all my emotions are on that beach with Gil.

Charley and Flint are silent. The occasional sob erupts from my lips. Then Charley's voice speaks gently in my mind. '*He loves you too.*'

I take a few deep breaths to try and calm myself.

'*He loves you.*'

She finally understands.

I nod. '*I know.*'

CHAPTER 40

The letter arrives the day we read about the explosion. The Disciples have done it: they've taken out the Kendrick facility. I read the British news online. The media aren't calling it the Kendrick facility; instead they report a new industrial complex in the Midlands was blown up. It's a miracle no one was hurt, but the explosion happened at night, and the security guards were given a ten-minute tip-off to get out of the area. Two hours later, the Disciples claimed responsibility for it. They are calling it the Kendrick facility. In an amazing act of denial, the police are insisting the Disciples are trying to take advantage of a gross act of vandalism. They have nothing to do with it.

'Unbelievable,' I say, shaking my head.

'*Incroyable*,' Flint says, showing off his increasing French vocabulary.

'What have we got for breakfast today?' Charley asks.

We live in a very small flat above a boulangerie. The smell of bread wafts up to us in the morning. One of us will go down to pick up either a crusty long baguette or, as a treat, croissants or a *petit pain* for breakfast. This morning, to honour the Disciples, we go for croissants.

'To Gil,' Charley says, raising her cup of coffee.

We all cheers that.

I look at the letter addressed to me on the table. It's got a British postmark. It makes me nervous. Charley and Flint grow quiet watching me.

'I think it's from Mary,' I say slowly. 'Tom promised me they'd let her know I was still alive. That if possible they might be able to pass on a letter.'

'Okay,' Flint says.

I pick it up and notice my hands are shaking. 'Shit,' I whisper. 'She might be saying goodbye.'

Charley shakes her head. 'I don't think so.'

'Read it in private,' Flint suggests.

'Yeah.'

I go into their bedroom. I sleep on the sofa in the living-room-cum-kitchen area, so their bedroom is private. I open the envelope carefully and pull out the few sheets of paper inside. It's Mary's handwriting.

Dearest Dom,

You are alive! The news filled my heart with such joy I thought it might burst. I just want to know that you are well and happy, and if you ache for anything it is only that you miss me, because you love me, as I miss and love you, and ache for you.

We are well. They interviewed us. It wasn't easy, and at one point they told Dad they had a recording of him talking to you about the D. I have never been so terrified but Dad kept his nerve. He told them to play the recording – but they didn't. Mostly, he shouted about what a terrible boyfriend you'd been and how glad we were to see the back of you. I think they were relieved to release us. Since then, everything has been calm.

Dom, there is so much I want to say, and yet somehow words seem inadequate. I know you cannot tell me when you will return, but I know you will.

I shall be waiting for you.

We shall be waiting for you.

I love you, always,

Mary

I close my eyes and feel the most intense relief. She loves me. She's waiting. Although MI5 interrogated them, they're alright; they've not been harmed. And with the *We* she wrote, I understand that Gregory too forgives me and accepts me. They're both waiting for me as I'm waiting to join them.

There's a second sheet of paper behind her letter. I look at it. It's a strange black-and-white image, like some picture from far away in outer space. A funnel shape and a slightly alien form. I get up and go back into the main room. Charley and Flint watch my face, judging my mood.

'I'm good.' I smile.

They both smile back. I can tell they're relieved.

'I don't get what this is,' I say, holding out the page with the image on it. I go and put it on the table. They look at it a while.

'Oh, my God,' Charley says. 'Oh, my God,' she repeats, a slight shake in her voice.

'What?' I ask. 'What is it?'

'I think it's what they call a three-month scan.'

'A three-month scan?' I say, bemused.

Flint and Charley exchange glances. Then Flint claps his hands together and laughs. 'You're going to be a father, Dom.'

I look at them, speechless.

Charley starts to giggle, she can't stop.

I stand there feeling shock then joy. Panic. Exhilaration. And finally, I laugh too.

ACKNOWLEDGEMENTS

Writing and publishing Eagle Heart has been a mountain to climb. I would like to thank the following for helping me reach the summit.

My editor, Lesley Jones, for her sound advice and attention to detail. Charlotte Coppack for the proofread and encouragement.

Jane Dixon Smith for designing a cover that catches so well the power of Eagle Heart.

The Alliance of Independent Authors for being a treasure trove of information and advice.

And, last but not least, thank you to my husband Paul whose timely suggestions helped me leap over the crevices that challenged me along the way.

ABOUT THE AUTHOR

SHONA BLASS was born in Glasgow and grew up in London. She wrote stories before she could read, and has been writing them ever since. She studied in Manchester and London. She lives in the New Forest with her husband. *Eagle Heart* is her second published novel, and the sequel to *Kingfisher*.

To find out more visit: www.shonablass.com